BORDER LESS

PRAISE FOR *BORDER LESS*

"An excellent, exciting debut, a novel that is not afraid to go into dangerous spaces and ask difficult questions. *Border Less* reimagines the experience of migration in powerful, surprising, and memorable ways."

—Chitra Banerjee Divakaruni, American Book Award winner and author of *The Last Queen*

"*Border Less* is a novel that invites the reader into the twists, turns, and corkscrews of immigrant life. From call centers in India to affluent eateries in Orange County, CA, these characters are irreverent, sometimes raunchy, anxiety-ridden, but most of all, explorative. Poddar has a sensitive touch to moving between time, space, and generations to present a continuous portrait of adventures and hardships in a racialized Brown body."

—Morgan Jerkins, *New York Times* bestselling author of *This Will Be My Undoing*

"*Border Less* is an intricate, dazzling tapestry that pulls threads from past and present—from Mumbai to California—crossing and blending stories and lives. Dia Mittal forges her way, inspired by and respectful of the generational dances, while also discovering her own path as she seeks that 'ethereal family reunion.' In this novel, Namrata Poddar keeps her eye on the individual heart while painting the most expansive orbit; she is a masterful writer, bringing time and place to life with vivid story and color and memorable wisdom."

—Jill McCorkle, *New York Times* bestselling author of *Hieroglyphics*

"Namrata Poddar delves with heartbreaking delicacy and precision into the solitary struggles of her characters, whether in the teeming, sweat-drenched Mumbai metropolis or on sunny Californian shores: through the tiny yet deep epiphanies that close each chapter of their lives, she shows us how every woman is borderless, with minds reaching out well beyond their shores and bodies enclosed within rigid confines. 'We are all migrants as soon as we are born,' reflects one of her characters. But women are even more so as they try to hold on to their center, to their core, while being pulled in different directions by the dictates of family, society, lovers, husbands, children. Until one day—one hopes—the ferociously unique kundalini awakens and takes her due."

—Ananda Devi, author of *Eve Out of Her Ruins,* winner of the Prix des cinq continents de la francophonie

"*Border Less* challenges the traditional form and aesthetic of the Western novel with a narrative of interconnected stories as layered as the human experience itself. Each of the novel's carefully drawn chapters explores questions of belonging and identity, complicated by geographic, racial, gender, and class distinctions, to name a few. Poddar is an ambitious and important new voice in the tapestry of global literature."

—Aline Ohanesian, author of *Orhan's Inheritance*, finalist for The Dayton Literary Peace Prize

"Namrata Poddar is a fierce storyteller, and *Border Less* has a lively, singular cast of characters that burn in the memory."

—Angie Cruz, author of *Dominicana*, and Editor-in-Chief of Aster(ix)

"*Border Less* is a serious transnational, feminist, and postcolonial novel. It is a deeply moving narrative of a migrant's journey from Mumbai to Southern California and her displacements over multiple spaces and her moments of self-discovery. This is a novel that finally gives voice to the complexity of being brown and a woman juggling the intersections of class, race, gender, nationality, and place."

—Reshmi Dutt-Ballerstadt, Professor of English at Linfield University, and author of *The Postcolonial Citizen*

"Namrata Poddar's *Border Less* is a dazzling debut! The promise of each character, who appears through vignettes, is to take you through a Mumbai you only thought you knew. Poddar's characters emerge from crevices in the city and they cross borders of class and convention, driven by ambition, imagination, and necessity. With the ladies special train commuter, you wonder, 'Who plays the central character and who becomes the footnotes in that fragmented city with a hollow center?' But the existential question that is cleverly posed becomes: do you have to see your blood spring from your body and taste it to look beyond the aggrieved resignation in the endless crowds of which you are a part? Pieces of the novel's puzzle gradually come together in the plot, which stretches from India through Mauritius to California. Characters are thrown up in a narrative that mirrors their intractability or tedium: a Nepali maid cooped up in a glass kitchen with the hopes of paying for her father's surgery; Dia who wants to be more Indian in her heart than in her habits; cousins whose separate lives across continents allow no reconciliation except in the rhythm of a childhood dance unforgotten by their bodies; immigrant parents and their American children negotiating family, home, love, and that elusive Dream. With a light hand but profound insight, sympathy, and humor, Poddar explores the new versions of gender and hierarchies that play out for different generations and different versions of 'Indians' in the US. With this auspicious inception, she experiments with hybrid literary genealogies, giving us a novel of poetic form and sensibility."

—Anjali Prabhu, Professor and Director of Comparative Literary Studies, Wellesley College, and author of *Hybridity: Limits, Transformations, Prospects*

"Pitch perfect and beautifully written, this debut novel of dislocation, belonging, and return captures with acuity and a light touch our shared transnational present and complex human ties."

—Françoise Lionnet, Professor of Comparative Literature at Harvard University, and author of *Postcolonial Representations: Women, Literature, Identity*

"Namrata Poddar's *Border Less* attempts to advance that evolution for a new generation of immigrants and their children, for whom South Asia and the United States aren't diametrically opposed but rather interconnected through mutual exchange. … In its tangle of "Roots" and "Routes"—its complementary halves—Poddar's debut sheds light on the inextricable networks that make up cosmopolitan India, its California spinoffs, and the cyclical, multigenerational journey from there to here and back again."

—**Meena Venkataramanan,** ***The Los Angeles Times***

"[A] Story that is made whole through its fragmentation. A thoughtful exploration of what it means to belong."

—**Wendy J. Fox,** ***BuzzFeed News***

"Illuminating debut … The range of perspectives harnessed announces Poddar as an exciting new voice in immigrant fiction."

—***Publishers Weekly***

"Not only does this resonant feminist debut challenge normative narratives of immigrant life, it also disrupts the notion of the Western novel in form and function."

—**Karla J. Strand,** ***Ms. Magazine***

"Namrata Poddar … has created an engaging debut by bringing us into the lives of those who leave and those who stay. If she is tilling familiar ground, she is also giving us a new set of characters. That the individual stories in *Border Less* can stand on their own is testament to her literary dexterity."

—**Martha Anne Toll,** ***NPR***

"The insights of Indian American diasporic experiences—where the borders of internalized colonialism and patriarchy are crossed and reinforced both ways—gives Poddar's literary effort its strength."

—**Gabriel San Román,** ***The Los Angeles Times: Times OC***

"Eschews mainstream literary convention to stand proudly as a work that makes its own rules."

—**Alice Stephens,** ***Washington Independent Review of Books***

"Nuanced shades of brownness burst into life in the pages of Namrata Poddar's *Border Less*, a literary exploration of migration that brings together characters as endearing as they are complex: the Nepali housemaid who finds subtle ways of rebelling against her employer, the Californian surgeon who tries to educate his mother about sexism while remaining oblivious to his own blind spots, and the young émigré who cannot, despite all her efforts, reconnect with the cousins who remained on the motherland. As it roves across cities and deserts, lingering on the centuries-old frescoes that immortalize the stories of the Thar Desert, *Border Less* is itself nothing less than a lustrous and colorful tapestry of migration in an imperfectly globalized world."

—Nikhita Obeegadoo, *Catapult*

"This is an immigrant story and the reader, no matter their heritage, will recognize similarities in family stories."

—Joan Curbow, *Booklist*

"The story signals a unique approach to migration and movement."

—Torsa Ghosal, *Los Angeles Review of Books*

"Gorgeous symphony of a novel that challenges so many preconceived notions of form."

—Grace Singh Smith, *Cleaver*

"There's much to admire about *Border Less*: the bold risks it takes with narration and structure, its carefully constructed layers, the depth of character revealed in a tight space, and its examination of what it means, and costs, to belong. But perhaps its most impressive virtue is its staunch rejection of the measurements the white Western canon uses to judge literature and its confident demand to be read on its own terms."

—Rachel León, *The Rupture*

"A multi-vocal exploration of a South Asian community stretching from Mumbai to Mauritius to California, and the ways in which these places and voices are depicted is a real highlight of the book."

—Rashi Rohatgi, *Brown Girl Magazine*

"*Border Less* ... spans the relationships of families, romances, friendships. It spans physical distances, across deserts and coasts and the globe. It spans generations, cultures, class, religion, gender, all creating that broad tapestry of interconnected experience."

—Winslow Schmelling, *Hayden's Ferry Review*

"Story by story, Poddar links the characters together, widening the circle until it encompasses the entire world and much of womanhood. ... The stories lash out at the patriarchy, particularly the last one, 'Kundalini,' which evokes the anger of the goddess. Yet, in this expanse of alienation and frustration, there are moments of tenderness and grace. Through it all, women compromise, bide their time, and build a life, longing for the day when they and the goddess will rise. But first, their stories must be told. *Border Less* does that with distinction."

—Raji Pillai, *India Currents*

"Questions mainstream modes of storytelling. Her style, which seems to draw on oral traditions, emphasizes repetition, rhythm, and reinvention."

—Khabar

"Poddar's novel is a pivotal debut of new writers honing in on the South Asian diaspora, but what makes her novel unique and a must-read is because she explores the gray areas of migration and identities that are a by-product of it—where one always belongs to the liminal space, always and forever in search for a home—for a place to belong."

—Nidhi Shrivastava, Professor of English at Sacred Heart University, and bookstagrammer

BORDER LESS

A NOVEL

NAMRATA PODDAR

HarperCollins *Publishers* India

First published in the United States of America by 7.13 Books in 2022
This edition published in India by HarperCollins *Publishers* 2022
4th Floor, Tower A, Building No. 10, Phase II, DLF Cyber City,
Gurugram, Haryana – 122002
www.harpercollins.co.in

2 4 6 8 10 9 7 5 3 1

P ISBN: 978-93-5629-022-8
E ISBN: 978-93-5629-023-5

Earlier versions of chapters in this book have appeared in the following publications: "Help Me Help You" in *The Kenyon Review*; "Silk Stole" in *Jaggery*; "Ladies Special" in *Lowestoft Chronicle*; "Tradeoff " in *The Bangalore Review*; "9/12" in *Literary Orphans*; "Anchor" in *The Missing Slate*; "Chutney" in *The Best Asian Short Stories 2019* (Kitaab, Singapore); "Excursion" in *Necessary Fiction*; "Nature, Nurture" in *The Feminist Wire*; "Blue and Brown" in *The Aerogram*; and "Victorious" in *New Asian Writing*.

Printed and bound at
Thomson Press (India) Ltd

For Ananya and Shome

Everywhere that the obligation to get around the rule of silence existed a literature was created that has no "natural" continuity, if one may put it that way, but, rather, bursts forth in snatches and fragments.

"Being is relation": but Relation is safe from the idea of Being.

—*Poetics of Relation*, Édouard Glissant,
translated by Betsy Wing

CONTENTS

ROOTS

ROUTES

ROOTS

HELP ME HELP YOU

DIA COVERED HER MOUTH so the American wouldn't hear her yawn. Last hour of answering calls before hitting home, switching shifts with Ma to take care of Papa, prepping for college finals, and returning to work the following night. She'd multitasked before, she'd done nightshifts for five years now, she could totally do this last hour, she told herself while parroting their airline's policy. "Yes Sir, you may carry two pieces of luggage for free, each weighing fifty pounds or under."

"Are you from Bangalore?" he asked. One of those drunk customers again, smitten with exotic women. And Chaya, her supervisor at Voizone call center, was keeping a strict watch on her performance. One week left in May and Dia had already exhausted her monthly limit of fatal errors over calls. With a toddler and an infant at home, Chaya could relate to her sleep deprivation. That wouldn't stop her from barging into Dia's phone conversations anytime.

"From Mumbai, Sir." Dia kept her answers short and rotated her shoulders, hard as stone from the absence of dance workouts she usually did before reporting to work. She looked at the clock on the computer screen ahead.

"Your voice is so sweet."

"Thank you, Sir. Have I answered all your travel questions?"

It had been thirteen minutes with the drunkard, three minutes past the ideal query resolution time. If the screen timer reached fifteen minutes, she'd get another fatal error on her monthly performance and would have to say goodbye to the promotion offer in Manila, her game plan out of Mumbai's survival rut and into the American dream with Aziz.

She stretched an arm sideward, rotated her wrist, and curled her middle finger into a Kathak mudra while the others pointed to Aziz, sitting in the cubicle across from her. The hand gestures from her training in dance worked as a code between them when they answered calls. Between their chairs, steel-grey carpeting divided rows of grey cubicles on each side of the room, reminders of American professionalism and productivity. Above them, a freshly painted ceiling, as if its golden yellow could infuse life into the drone of buzzing telephones, the sea of hunched backs, and the second-by-second monitored performance of a Third World sucking up to the First.

Aziz swiveled his chair toward Dia and lip-synched. *Everything okay?*

"Are you wearing a sari?" the customer asked.

"No, Sir." Dia jutted her tongue out and raised a thumb toward her mouth.

Aziz peeked through Chaya's door, close to his side of the room. He'd figured how to tell if Chaya was in. Between the door and the wall, there was a crack through which he could spot the metal knob when the door was locked.

"What are you wearing then?"

Aziz nodded toward their office's back exit. Chaya was out for a Shanti break, snacking on marijuana cookies sold illegally at the paanwallah's stall across from their office building, Voizone's open secret to surviving the night shifts, the sleep deprivation, the social isolation, the cameras, the clocks, the Americans.

Dia rotated her other palm and brought her index finger to lightly touch her thumb. Aziz winked at her and returned to his call.

"Sir, I've resolved your query and am not allowed to answer personal questions. Do not hesitate to call us again should you have an airline-related query. Thank you and have a great day." She hung up and looked at the computer. Fourteen minutes, thirty-five seconds, read the large clock on the screen below a map of the United States along with several smaller clocks with three highlighted in red—New York, Chicago, and Los Angeles, homes to business schools topping her wishlist, Stern, Kellogg, Anderson. *Array, if you get into any of these, you're set for life*, she'd heard from senior colleagues.

Her phone rang again. "Dia here for Hansa Airlines. How may I help you?"

With college finals, May was usually a tough month at work for Dia, but she'd managed to make it so far. This, though, was her last year at college so the pressure to do well in exams was higher; the scores would be crucial for getting into an MBA program. She and Aziz had planned this for months. Both came from lower-middle-class backgrounds, both knew life in survival mode—a staple for many Mumbaikers including their Voizone colleagues. They had a good ability in switching accents, reason they'd had more success with Voizone clients than other agents with thicker accents, especially those from rural India. Aziz had even bagged April's Agent of the Month award, a way for him to vouch for Dia's promotion to Chaya. If they persisted for a few more months at work, they were most likely to get nominated as supervisors for Voizone's branch in Manila, a position with double the salary, daytime hours, and a regular social life. Three years in Manila and bingo—enough savings to start an MBA program in the U.S. and a better life abroad. By the time Dia entered her fifth year at Voizone, the stars had seemed aligned in the couple's favor until two months back when her father had a relapse of throat cancer, forcing him to take a break from his job and leaving Dia as the sole provider for their family. His recovery from chemo was taking longer than expected and college finals were here. To cope, Dia cut back on dance workouts, her zen place as she often called it, so she could win time for exam prep at home and give Ma a breather from taking care of Papa.

Upon returning from work to their one-bedroom flat, Dia insisted that Ma sleep in the living room where Dia usually slept. Being well-rested was the best way she could help both Papa and Dia that time of the year. In the kitchen, she opened a foldable recliner and decided to take a nap too before more studying. Five more days of finals and she would check a Bachelor of Commerce off her list, that useless, non-negotiable degree to qualify for most jobs she knew, from a peon's post in Mumbai to a call-center gig in Manila or grad school in the U.S.

The sound of someone walking from the toilet toward the bedroom jolted her awake. "Papa, wait!" She rushed to her father, ghostly in a white kurta-pajama too big for his reedlike body. She wrapped an arm around his waist and slipped her shoulder below his. "Didn't I tell you to wake me up whenever you've got to go?" She controlled the irritation in her voice. Two weeks before, he'd lost balance and slipped in the shower, spraining his ankle. The third round of chemo had drained him. They couldn't afford another fall.

"I'm doing better now." His hand trembled on her shoulder.

"Of course, you are. Few more days of precaution though, please?"

"Want you to get some sleep." He steadied himself on the bed's mattress. "Your finals—"

"Five more days. Then I can sleep as much as I want." She supported his back as he lay down. "If I'd slept through the morning, I would've screwed up anyway. Need to be done with Econ notes today." She covered him with a blanket, fighting the urge to tell him she had a Muslim boyfriend. She could so use Aziz's help at home.

"You're my Durga, you know?" her father said. And she wondered what had taken root in his shaky voice—resignation toward cancer or guilt at not playing the provider. If the news weren't flooded with ISIS threats to the U.S. or Indo-Pak tension in Kashmir, she would've confessed about Aziz right then.

"Me clearly no Sita," she said, switching off the light in the bedroom. In the kitchen, she pulled out a can of Titana she'd hidden in the recliner's side pocket. It was an American energy drink that Aziz had introduced her to when she was first adapting to night shifts at Voizone. One can equaled nearly five cups of coffee but didn't give her the stomach ulcers like over-consumption of caffeine did. Her parents knew Titana to be one of those tasteless foreign sodas that youngsters loved; she never told them otherwise. She opened her Economics textbook and took a big sip from her can. In ten minutes, she would crack these demand-supply fuckers, she told herself while staring into a pair of sleep-inducing graphs.

Two days left for the month of May and a last exam to go. Dia had managed to stay functional at work. She helped care for Papa at home who was getting better by the day and fared reasonably well in her college finals too. Twenty more hours of answering calls at Voizone to cover her monthly quota, although something in her body told her she'd need to do more that evening to stay alert. On her way to work, she stopped by Groove dance studio.

Dhoom machalayyy, Sunidhi Chauhan crooned from the main hall's massive stereo system at Groove. Dia undulated her torso, dropped, and raised her shoulders in a semicircular motion to the beat. To the chorus, she rotated her belly clockwise and counter-clockwise, then repeated the same with her chest, hips, and hands. Sweat trickled down her torso, wetting her hip scarf studded with fake gold coins. As she jumped high, then squatted on her feet, and jumped high again with her troupe, she felt the lightness release the tension in her upper body. Her eyes felt so fresh with the rush of oxygen, she could totally manage four hours of sleep a night for two more days and get to the month of June. *Dhoom machalay dhoom machalay dhoom.* She kneeled and touched her palms to the floor in a closing pose, watching her chest rise and fall in jerky exhales.

On her way out, she waved goodbye at her coach who held up a brochure, reminding her of the Bollywood gig where he would choreograph a movie starring Rutik Roshan; Dia would be such an asset to his troupe. The coach knew how much she disliked her job answering calls at Voizone. He kept telling her how dance could be more than a hobby, a real career, if only she'd risk what she truly wanted. "The offer hasn't expired!" he yelled while her phone beeped. Aziz's text; he was on his way to work and would pick her up at the shuttle stop. "The girl's got plans," she said, her usual response. He meant well but she knew enough Bollywood junior artists to know how unreliable their paychecks were. She might not enjoy faking a Yankee accent at work or any of her courses at business school as much as she enjoyed pirouetting to a Bollywood number but she did know this: she wanted a life with freedom of choice, including the pursuit of happiness, that classic American ideal, and the freedom to choose seldom came with an empty wallet.

The shuttle pulled up. She climbed in and sat next to Aziz.

"If you went to Voizone gym instead of Groove, you'd save thirty minutes and catch up on sleep," he said.

"Worth every second, this time away from the jail," she said. Diesel fumes from a truck blackened the windows of their air-conditioned shuttle.

"The jail is our passport to freedom, remember?" As if her coach weren't enough, Aziz started his usual pep talk too. If she slept better, she'd stay more alert at calls. He pulled her toward him. "We're this close to the American dream, jaan."

"We shall overcome." Her head cocked back and forth in a figure eight, just like Rutik did in that song in *Natarajan*, her latest Bollywood favorite.

Aziz looked deep into her eyes and said in a soft voice, "Just trying to cheer you up."

That gaze, so full of desire, so empty of doubt. How she loved Aziz for his clarity of vision, how she hated him for his easy trust. Of course, he bagged Agent of the Month. Aziz whined his share about call-center life as well, the sleep deprivation, the clocks, the clientele, and other usual suspects, but he *would* overcome. His parents were lower middle class too. Neither had had cancer though, and they had another son and an extra income.

"Tired," she said, resting her head on his shoulder. "Besides, taking the shuttle thirty minutes later means I get to dance and I get to chat with you. Win-win."

After taking her college exam, Dia entered Voizone on the last evening of May. She tiptoed from the elevator toward her office's entrance and signed her name on the attendance sheet.

"Late again." Chaya stood behind her.

Dia bit her lip, turned around, and apologized. It wouldn't happen again. With her dad's recovery and final exams, it had been a tough month, she reminded her supervisor.

Chaya raised an eyebrow. Dia looked away. In the room adjoining the main hall, a new group of interns received training. Abuse management, the whiteboard read. Two columns separated the board; one read *Americans, aggressive, efficient, small talk*; another read *Indians, polite, listeners, X*. The trainer's wooden ruler pointed at X. A few eager hands went up.

"Ms. Dia Mittal," Chaya said. "I'd love to play tragedy queen with you but your performance report is due in two days. How the hell will you cover your quota for today?" Chaya reminded her about the fatal errors she'd committed for the month, the remaining quota of calls she needed to hit that day, sixty total, no joke unless she was highly alert, effective, and downright lucky with the nature of customer queries.

Chaya rubbed her fake leather belt. "With your ability to switch accents, you're one of our best players for Manila," Chaya said, leaning toward her, careful not to be heard by others. "You get that job, I get promoted to better hours too." That's how it worked at their office. Every senior nominated a junior for promotion, and with the qualifying junior, the respective supervisor got priority in choosing their hours for work.

"It's been really—"

"Trust me, dahling. I want you out of here more than you do. So help me help you."

Dia blinked.

"Help. Me. Help. You." Chaya pulled her elbows toward her waist and squatted like Jerry Maguire. When Dia had started working for Voizone, Chaya had screened the movie at orientation week to emphasize how different their life as an agent was to Jerry's. As she saw Chaya's palms quiver, she knew Chaya had had an extra dose of Shanti.

"Yes, Ma'am." Dia nodded and walked to her cubicle. It would be pointless talking further. Chaya wanted more time with her children as much as Dia wanted Manila. Chaya and her husband divorced a year back, and rumor had it that their lawyer's bill had stripped her of every day care option.

Dia finished resolving her customer Rebecca's query in an impressive two-and-a-half minutes. Rebecca then asked her where she was really from. When Dia said India, Rebecca told her about her stay in Rajasthan learning miniature paintings, visiting havelis, camel-riding on sand dunes. She went to Jaipur, where she'd met her husband. It was one of those calls that eased the constant pressure to perform in their voice business—anecdotes from Americans who seemed genuinely nice, and knew the difference between India and Indonesia.

"I want to show them the Pink City where they were

conceived," Rebecca told Dia about her four-year-old twins and the next planned family trip to India over the Christmas break.

"Ideal weather to visit, Ma'am." Dia looked at the numbers changing on her computer screen.

"We got so lucky with our reservations."

"Great." Four more hours and twenty-three calls to finish her weekly quota, doable if she stayed focused. "Is there anything else I can help you with?"

"That'll be all, sweetheart. Thank you, and oh…Namaste."

"Namaste." She hung up, pulled a Sprite bottle out of her handbag, and took large sips of Titana.

Seventy-five minutes of work left for the month of May. Seven more calls after which Dia would sleep like a baby, and if the Goddess stayed by her side, qualify for the Manila gig. She massaged her temples and her forehead. No more than ten minutes per call, she told herself, fighting the urge to close her eyes. Her phone rang again.

Vicky was the customer. "We have a situation here," she said. She'd selected and confirmed her seats for a trip to Paris while buying tickets online with Hansa but when she logged into her account to enter her meal preference, the airline asked for an additional $35 toward confirming seats for each connecting flight. "The only reason I got this $400 ticket was because I was getting a deal with confirmed seats. And now, Hansa is trying to rip me off by charging extra."

"Sorry to hear, Ma'am," Dia said, typing. She asked Vicky the basic security questions and logged into her account. "My computer screen is showing your seats as unconfirmed." She knew Hansa had recently introduced the $35 surcharge for seat reservations. Like other airlines, it was their way to make up for the rise in gas prices.

"But I saw my seats confirmed earlier, here on my screen."

She asked Vicky to log out and log in again. She did the same at her end. Now both their accounts were showing Vicky's seats as unconfirmed.

"I'm so disappointed," Vicky said. "Not my fault if you introduced a fee for seats. I'd purchased the ticket before your new rule. Unfair of Hansa to make me pay for seats now." She asked Dia to waive the fee. Dia remembered the recent warning to Voizone agents—they needed to be careful with customers claiming all sorts of refunds; agents could allow these only after seeing documented evidence in the form of an email receipt or a screenshot of an order confirmation. Chaya's tone had been as imperial as Vicky's.

"This must be really frustrating for you, Ma'am." Dia modulated her tone for empathy as agents were trained to. "Can you email me the e-ticket showing your seats as confirmed?"

"I've lost my e-ticket, that's why I'm calling you. When I first logged into my account, the screen showed my seats as confirmed—" Vicky repeated her story.

Dia repeated their airline's new policy. "To sanction a waiver, I need to see a proof of your seats as confirmed." She kept her eyes on the screen. Following the courtesy opening, the case summary, the logins and logouts, she'd two more minutes to hit the ideal query resolution time of fifteen minutes. If she missed this, she'd have an additional fatal error that she'd managed to avoid the whole of May.

"Can Hansa waive my fee for seat reservations?" Vicky repeated. "It's only fair."

"I understand, Ma'am." Dia looked at the seconds running on the screen, ninety left. These things happened; but without a written proof, she didn't have the authority to sanction a waiver. Chaya did. If she could transfer Vicky's call to her supervisor, she could come in under the ideal query resolution time. "Let me see what we can do. May I put you on hold as I connect you to my supervisor?"

"You may *not*," Vicky said. "I've spent an hour on the phone already with this, talking to you, and before that, the nightmarish wait to get connected to a human being, not a voicemail, and you want to put me on hold again for something that isn't even my fault? Why don't you call me back like my T-Mobile customer service does?"

Dia exhaled. Fifty-five seconds. "I'm afraid the moment this call gets disconnected, you'll be transferred to another agent and the case will be treated afresh. I'm sure my supervisor can help you, Ma'am."

"Because you cannot. None of you can, quite frankly. It's always passing the line from one person to another to another before the customer finally gives up." Vicky was speaking faster, the pitch of her voice higher. "That's why talking to Indians is so useless. You are lazy—and slow—and the whole system is so disorganized, and then you steal our jobs. You know, I really don't want to be mean here but my son worked very hard at his IT job, building America's mobile network and bringing it where it is—"

Dia looked at her screen, her heart beating faster. Seventeen seconds. "And now you guys barge in, and because of you, he's lost his job and it's all so unfair—" Vicky kept going. Five, four, three, two, one. As Dia stared at the zero blinking on her screen, a ringing in her ear drowned the noise around her, including Vicky's rant. Manila was officially off the charts for now.

"Hello?" Vicky said.

Dia looked at the cubicle next to hers. Aziz's empty chair. He'd finished his shift and was hanging at Zen for happy hour.

"Helloooo. Are you with me?"

"I'm not, Your Highness. Find another sucker for your racist bullshit." Dia disconnected the call. She removed her headphones and placed them between her teeth, feeling the rush of energy throughout her body. Was it her voice that felt so calm and confident? Her phone rang again; it was Chaya.

Upon entering Chaya's office, Dia apologized immediately. She was sorry for Chaya and her children. It wasn't her intention, single parenting is tough, of course she understood, but Vicky was being mean and she was trying to deal with her in a dignified way, the way they were taught at the abuse management seminar.

"But Vicky. Isn't. The. Fucking. Point. Dahling." Chaya cut through her monologue.

"The point then?" Dia asked.

"Irate behavior management. *Empathy* as response." Chaya bent her neck toward each shoulder forcefully, as if trying hard to stay alert. "That was the point of the seminar last month."

Dia sucked her cheeks in.

"A customer is angry, you listen, you let them vent, then you offer words of empathy."

"Like, sincere apologies for stealing your jobs. We, the descendants of Apu, will try harder to reform ourselves?" she said, despite herself.

"Make an effort, dammit." Chaya slapped a file against her table. "We have the record of your response in writing."

"I don't get it," Dia said. "Last month, you were training us to be more assertive in the abuse management seminar."

Chaya cupped her nape with her palm and massaged her mid-shoulder muscles. "I've worked pretty hard training those guys to get their accent right." She raised her chin toward the room where interns from Ahmedabad were getting inducted. "An entire week spent on getting dee-vel-up-ment right instead of dav-il-up-ment. Some common sense on your part and you could've gotten the Manila gig. Americans are aggressive as we *all* know." Chaya's hand seemed to slice the tabletop. "The reason India is excelling on the outsourcing front is because we provide excellent value to Americans with our courtesy and patience. By building the right rapport, you would've done both you and your country a huge service—"

"And a service to you, let's not forget," Dia said. How easily Chaya had reversed her spiel after that seminar. *Remember, agents, we're here to provide service to the Americans. But we can do this without being doormats.*

Chaya picked up her file and put it on the shelf beside her desk. "Idealism bhunkuss," she said. "And remind me, dahling, when are those chemo bills due?" She returned to checking her email. "Maybe Manila is better off without you. We need more than a Barbie accent there." She typed feverishly on her keyboard.

"Yes, Ma'am." Dia picked up her handbag and trudged toward her office's exit. "Good luck finding your puppet." She slammed the door.

Dia walked to Inorbit Mall, a commercial complex across from Voizone, and took the elevator up to Zen. She ordered a Narayan, one of Zen's bestselling shots made from a Caribbean rum that was 87% alcohol, and drank it in a gulp. Her ribcage burned. Her head felt lighter within minutes. She ordered a Kingfisher next and walked to the bar's open-air terrace. Aziz was chatting with colleagues, sipping a Kingfisher too, and looking particularly cheerful. She filled him in on Vicky's story and Chaya's refusal to understand. When she was done, he stayed silent, his head bobbing to the rhythm of Bhangra rap playing in the background.

"What?" she asked.

"I'm not Chaya's biggest fan," he said, "but talking back at customers wasn't what she was getting at last month." His shoulders moved up and down. "I mean, if a dog barks at you, you don't bark back."

"Naw. Therefore, ladies and gentlemen, and always." She raised her beer bottle toward him. "Buck up and suck up."

On the street below, cars honked, rickshaws beeped, buses grunted, adding their own rhythm to the bar's Bhangra beats. Behind the sea of traffic stood a row of eclectic shops, Groove dance studio, Voizone's shuttle stop, and the panwallah's kiosk, right by the entrance of Inorbit Mall.

Aziz modulated his voice for empathy as if Dia was his American customer and reminded her to stay focused on their dream. "It's not late to apologize to Chaya." He rubbed Dia's upper arm. "We can totally use that abuse management seminar in our defense, and she probably understands."

"I tried." She squinted at her empty bottle and turned it upside down. "And let's, for a moment, think it's all cool. Chaya's cool, forgives and forgets. I get the promo in six months, Dad's maha cool, gotten super healthy and stuff. I'm in Manila. Then what?"

"What do you mean, then what?"

"I mean, who's to know it'll get easier?" Dia kept staring in the direction of Groove sandwiched between a hardware and an upholstery store.

"We've talked about this for months, jaan!" Aziz threw his arms up in the air. "Not like we have a hundred options, do we? The best you can do is work with what you have."

The street below continued to bustle, teenage boys eve-teased, women haggled with street hawkers, exhausted dancers walked out of Groove. Everything from Zen's terrace seemed to point at the harmony below, as if there lay a secret rhythm to the chaos, visible only from an elevated space, accessible to a chosen few.

Aziz took the beer bottle from Dia's hand and placed it on the table next to them. "I got a five-week training offer in Boston." He lowered his voice and pushed a strand of hair behind her ear. "I know it's not the best time for this, but they need my answer by tomorrow. If I accept, I'll be leaving for Manila from there directly."

"Like, by tomorrow?"

"Like, tomorrow."

It was at Zen that she'd first met Aziz. It was over Voizone happy hours that their friendship had morphed into a strong chemical pull, an outlet from work. Over time, physical attraction had grown into something deeper. She'd grown used to the smell of his hair tidied with almond oil, the salt in his sweat, the weight and the wet of him on her, the deep grunt with which his body quaked before coming; she'd grown used to their shared dream of a life in the U.S., a life beyond call centers once they'd saved enough from their senior positions in Manila. How often they'd talked about watching a Lakers or Dodgers game live, about shopping at IKEA where all of Voizone furniture came from, about American MBA programs that were less about memorizing books, more about socializing and networking, Penn State and Ohio State had amazing football teams, you could actually see the Hollywood sign from a UCLA building, and California produce! The strawberries were huge. Even lemons there were the size of grapefruit! The USA they faked knowing, they would experience together someday—Niagara Falls, the Statue of Liberty, the Grand Canyon; they would actually fly Hansa Airlines.

"You'll take it, yes?" she said. Of course she wanted him to accept the training offer. She knew how much he needed the money too. He'd recently spent a fortune getting the ceiling fixed for his folks in Navi Mumbai so it wouldn't leak during the monsoons.

"In Manila, I'll work my contacts—"

Dia raised her chin, held back tears. "Just want to be alone for a bit." She picked up her purse.

"Jaan." He followed her.

"Not now." She walked toward the escalator going down. As she passed through the mall's revolving exit door, Mumbai reeled around her—taxis honking, rickshaws beeping, the buses poisoning the city with diesel fumes, kids trotting to school, holding their parent's hand, and beyond, Groove, where her coach was probably training his troupe for Rutik. Aziz would leave for Manila after Boston and she wouldn't see him for three years. In her turn, she'd officially entered Chaya's bad books. Even if Aziz pulled a few strings and she had the Manila offer in a few months, there was always the question of Papa's chemo and a relapse. Maybe she'd take up her coach's offer on Bollywood. Dance would fill her cup alright but would it cover Papa's hospital bills? She'd never know until she risked what she truly wanted, but would she risk it? For five years, she'd faked an American accent over the phone. Could she *be* an American, though? Place the individual at the center of the drama, and write the story of her life based on what she alone wanted? Let her folks fend for themselves if it didn't work out? Confront her goddamn fears, risk the unknown, as her coach and Aziz often goaded her into doing? But for once, she didn't want to risk survival. For once, she wanted comfort, and ease, and stability in this city bursting with millions dreaming the same dream, in this city so tightfisted on luck and opportunity. For once, she wanted to stop her fucking mental chatter. Stop the noise inside her, outside of her, and all movement around her—the cars, the rickshaws, the trucks, the buses, the kids, the eve-teasers, the nagging voice of desire, doubt, and a First-World bhunkuss on life, liberty, and the pursuit of happiness she was inducted into that orientation week at Voizone. For once she wanted peace, lots and lots of it.

She walked to the panwallah's kiosk. She bobbed her head to a beat. *Dhoom machalayyy*. She rolled her shoulder and raised an arm, reaching her fingers toward the sky. As she slithered her arm down in slow motion, she rolled her other shoulder and raised the other arm. She undulated her limbs and her torso like a cobra hypnotized to the swirl of a snake charmer's flute. Her head quaked. *Dhoom machalay dhoom*. She strutted toward the panwallah, extended her right arm and her foot forward, then alternated the movement with her other arm and foot.

"Good office party, Madam?" the panwallah asked with a knowing smile.

She nodded and asked for Super Shanti, extra strong cannabis he secretly sold by mixing it in soft drinks. "In Sprite, Chacha." She extended a few hundred-rupee notes. With trembling hands and grinding teeth, she gulped down the soda, savoring the flow of its fiery bubbles corroding her larynx. She twirled toward the shuttle stop and saw the Voizone van approach. The ride back home in rush-hour traffic would last over an hour. She cha-cha-chaed to her seat, thumped her head against the window, and let super peace kick in.

SILK STOLE

JOOHI MITTAL'S NEIGHBORS LOVED to talk about the Almighty's mood swings. Poor Joohi, Mount Sinai duplex to Malava cubicle! From three maids to three-plus jobs! Supperware, delivery woman, stock market, housemaid, widowed mother of three. Kishan's chemo made the family total kadkaa yah. The game of His Maya, who can ever win?

Joohi let the neighbors talk as she walked out of a Malava building, adjusting the weight of her tote bag with its half-sold Supperware products on her shoulder. She had time enough for that monthly visit to her stockbroker before delivering the next round of tiffin boxes to a client celebrating her five-year-old's birthday.

The game of His Maya, who knew what next? Kishan, the love of her life, gone. The savings from selling their Mount Sinai duplex, gone. The savings from selling the two-hundred-year-old haveli of her own forefathers in Rajasthan, gone. Even her once-dark, voluminous curls were growing thinner by the day like her Supperware income.

She walked past Omega, Malava's latest all-purpose store dealing in half-priced Chinese duplicates of most of her products. The boxes in her tote poked the edge of her ribs. She felt grateful that at least a handful of her clients still appreciated the real deal.

One of her friend's stockbrokers had recently told her, "Infrastructure and technology—safest bet for your money, Joohi sister." Just as Kishan would tell his friends at their Mount Sinai parties where the boys would talk investment possibilities in Mumbai's construction boom and IT ventures.

She knew investing in Airavat, the corporate upstart backing the city's metro construction, would pay off, but a return this early! She walked out of the stockbroker's office, enjoying the bulge of crisp Gandhis, those large thousand-rupee notes, in her wallet. As she walked back home, she barely noticed the October heat.

After cooking, packing lunch, sending her children off for the day, she sank into her hall's sofa with a cup of masala chai. Usually, this was the time she would wash clothes by hand, dust furniture, sweep and mop her one-bedroom flat, start another round of Supperware delivery, or restock products for sale before her children returned when she would serve them dinner and help them with their homework. That day, she decided to make a shopping list instead—a careful investment plan that would pay off, just like Airavat. It had been a while since she'd spent a large sum of money. And she was a Marwari after all. Maybe that's where her true vocation lay? Investments. She opened the notebook where she kept an account of daily expenses. She took a loud slurp of chai.

Three thousand rupees she would invest in a writing desk for her five-year-old daughter, Soni. They had a foldable dining table that the boys used as a desk but it was too tall for Soni. So she would complete her homework by placing books on a serving tray over her lap and the books often toppled over. By keeping her back straight and her books steady, a desk would motivate her youngest to take her studies seriously. Another couple of thousands would go in a secondhand Samson tablet for Anay, her thirteen-year-old. Almost everyone in Anay's class had a tablet by now and his IT scores were lowering without steady practice. The tablet could also strengthen his desire toward an IT major, ensuring a lucrative career. For three thousand or so, Joohi would buy a suit for her eighteen-year-old, Rohit, as he was to interview soon for summer internship with banks. His old blazer had turned snug and his formal trousers looked a little short; he'd grown an inch in the last six months. Chances were he wouldn't grow anymore.

She added the expenses and had about four thousand left. She reached for her chai. Another contemplative slurp. She would invest the rest in getting her flat walls fixed. The paint was not only chipping in many parts but two walls in the hall were displaying amoebas of mold due to the rainwater leaking in. Instead of spending a bomb on home improvement, she would get creative. She would ask the handyman to apply a coat of waterproof primer on the walls and another coat of whitewash in return for a discounted rate and free Supperware boxes she'd received as a bonus from her boss last Christmas. She would then buy oil paint and create floral vines on the edge of the walls, inspired by her ancestral haveli in Rajasthan. Not a bad value for her rupee. She drank the last of her chai, savoring the aftertaste of ginger in entrepreneurial satisfaction.

She set out for Malava Market, waiting at the closest bus stop. Twenty minutes passed. The sun shone brutally, and the humidity drained her energy so she took a rickshaw: sixty rupees instead of five for the bus. Just today, she told herself, as she wiped the sweat trickling down her upper lip.

On its way to the crowded market, the rickshaw passed through Inorbit Mall, the latest branch of the chain opened in her side of the city. The windows displayed neon signs reading "Mega Sale" and "Diwali Clearance Sale." She asked the rickshaw wallah to stop.

As she entered Stop & Shop, a huge wave of air conditioning enveloped her. She sat on a bench by the accessories counter and reveled in the cool air. Soft instrumental music played across the store. The tunic and leggings sticking to her sweaty body started drying up. Her energy levels seemed to rise. She threw her elbows back, felt something soft and slippery, turned her head, and saw a blue-and-green stole by Rita Kumar, blockprinted with peacock and lotus motifs.

Rita Kumar had been her favorite designer in those Mount Sinai days. She remembered her last wedding anniversary with Kishan, two weeks before he died. His throat cancer had entered its terminal stage, and the doctors had politely advised them not to bother with chemo anymore. She'd already sold her ancestral house in Rajasthan to cover the hospital bills. As she sponged him in bed after dinner, he had surprised her with a Rita Kumar, a turmeric silk scarf blockprinted with delicate silver vines that gave an illusion of uniformity and continuity. So you hold on to a little luxury no matter how bad it gets, he'd said as he raised the scarf toward her neck with trembling hands. When she bent her head over his face, she didn't tell him she'd visited a real estate agent that morning to list their duplex flat for sale.

A placard above the display rack at Stop & Shop read "Up to 35% off." She raised the stole, ran a hand through it, and lifted the price tag. Three thousand eight hundred and fifty rupees was crossed out; another tag stuck on top of it reading 2499 Rs.

She placed the stole around her neck, caressing the fabric. A salesgirl came over. "The color looks so good on you, Ma'am," she said. No one had called Joohi "Ma'am" in a long time.

"Got any in pure silk?" Joohi asked, surprised by the authority in her voice. At Malava, the rare times Joohi shopped for her clothes were with street vendors at the station market. And fussing over cheap polyester when buying a two-hundred-rupee Kalvin Clain tunic would have been silly.

The girl bent over another rack and flipped open a few stoles: a yellow-purple, a red-green, an orange-pink. "Thirty-five percent off silk blends," she said, pointing to the colorful bunch in one hand. "Pure crêpe silk are 20% only."

Joohi picked up the orange-and-pink stole in pure crêpe silk. "I'll take it."

As she walked out carrying a handmade paper bag with Rita Kumar written in gold, she felt people's glances on her. She took the elevator to the restroom where she took off the price tag, circled the stole around her neck, and stroked the fabric with her fingers again. How good the touch of silk felt. And how the orange-pink accentuated her chai skin under the restroom's soft lights. She leaned into the mirror, waiting for the voices in her head to return.

Three children to take care of, Ram kasam. When God couldn't take care of everyone, he created a *mother.* Take the girl out of Mount Sinai but you can't take Mount Sinai out of the girl! You have to give us a discount on this Supperware bottle, Joohi sister. Omega selling the same for eighty rupees, I swear!

Joohi ignored the voices in her head. She pulled the rubber band out of her ponytail and tousled her hair. The woman in the silk stole standing in front of her seemed completely at ease with her purchase. And her overused beige tunic did not look cheap at all; it looked deliberately understated in an effort to highlight her stole's colors, her salt-and-pepper curls too. Joohi raised her chin and threw her shoulders back. The woman in the mirror winked at her.

On stepping out of the restroom, Joohi stopped by Grantha Book Shop. As if on reflex, she walked straight to the History section where a huge hardcover titled *Haveli Architecture and the Silk Road* was on display. She flipped through its images of opulent mansions covered in fresco paintings. When Kishan was running his textile business in their Mount Sinai days, she loved spending her afternoons reading books on the textile history of the Silk Road and the Thar Desert where her ancestral two-hundred-year-old haveli stood. Like many Marwaris from the Shekhawati region in Rajasthan, the couple's families had moved to Indian cities in the early 1900s. Mittal Haveli belonging once to her great-great-grandfather was the sole tangible link to their centuries-old history in the Thar Desert. It was where Joohi had chosen to get married as soon as she finished her bachelor's in history at the same university where Kishan was pursuing an MBA. The couple spent every Diwali at the haveli until Kishan got diagnosed.

The hardcover's price tag read 3150 Rs. Joohi ran her fingers through the mansion's windows with multiple frames on the cover page. She handed the cashier exact change and put another hundred and fifty in the charity box that read: Feed India.

It was half past two, and she was craving an afternoon snack. Across Grantha was Coffee Keen, one of those American chains of coffee shops gaining a monopoly across Mumbai. She ordered a cheese puff and a mango frappuccino. In their college days, Kishan had taken Joohi on their first date to StarLuck, the first Americanized café in Mumbai. How she'd fallen in love with their mocha frappuccino, the desserty cold coffee that had hit the spot after the couple's lunch at Rock-n-Roll where they'd enjoyed kathi rolls. When Kishan was on a liquid diet in his post-chemo days and crabby about drinking another vegetable juice, she'd bring him, on occasions, a StarLuck frappuccino customized with minimal sugar, glass half-full. While he sipped his beverage, she'd sit on his bed and cheer him with tales of their courtship night after night, often retelling the story of their first date, adding, embellishing, or altering details to distract him from his lack of appetite so he'd drink more and ingest more calories and stay alive. Since his death, she'd never entered an Americanized café. Things were outrageously expensive there anyway.

As she waited for her order at Coffee Keen, she noticed the huge glass windows surrounding the café as they blocked the air and noise pollution from the streets, letting light in. A strange feeling swelled within her, digging a void deeper. She blinked a few times, jerked her head, and told herself: here and now. Executives and college kids sat in the café, chitchatting, sipping drinks, or working on their laptops. She took off her stole, laid it on the table, and browsed through her book. The fragrance of coffee beans induced a certain calm in her. As she ate her cheese puff and sipped her frappuccino, she smiled at the college kid who was checking out her stole. When done, she left fifty rupees on the table for the server.

Across Coffee Keen stood a dimly lit room with a sign over

the doorway that read “Nilgiri Salon and Spa”. A bulletin board by the entrance flaunted the daily specials. “Hair Wash and Head Massage for 1800 Rs.” She opened her purse and stared at the remaining Gandhis, running her fingers through them, three times. She walked past the imposing electric fountain and lounging chairs toward the receptionist who asked her how she could be helped. She requested the day’s specials. A woman wearing a white apron and white-rimmed glasses took her to a lounging chair in front of a washbasin.

Women around her lounged in chairs too; a couple of them were talking on their smartphones, another played with her iPad, yet another was asking a staff girl for herbal tea. The girl in the white apron started washing her hair. She uncrossed her legs and sank into her chair. Buddha Bar music played in the background, and the spa smelled of subtle lavender candles. She focused on the forceful spray of warm water massaging her scalp. She tried to smell the fruits in the herbal shampoo, papaya, mango, melon, not wanting to miss any of the sensory pleasures.

When the girl in the white apron excused herself to bring oil for the head massage, a woman in the chair next to Joohi’s asked what time it was and started making conversation. They talked about Mumbai’s impossible traffic, the need to get home before rush hour began.

“Grocery shopping can be a *total* pain these days.” The woman pulled a Prada handbag closer to her chest and unzipped it. Two staff girls sat by her feet, giving her a pedicure. “I want to hit the road by four forty-five. The moment it’s five, this place turns into a zoo, doesn’t it?” The woman removed a slender tube of hand cream, squeezed some of it into her palm, and extended the tube to Joohi.

Joohi nodded. “I’m hoping to reach the market by four. They’ve opened another branch of Shah’s coaching class behind Malava Market. By four-thirty, imagine the college kids snacking by Khau Galli.” She helped herself to some hand cream.

"I meant Mega Mandee yah," the woman said, interlocking her palms in a circular massaging motion. She told Joohi about the huge grocery store that had opened behind Inorbit Mall. "Now with competition from Kay Mart, Mandee guys are offering free parking for an hour. And eight pay desks so lines never get that long."

Joohi rubbed her palms and brought them closer to her face. She wanted to tell the woman that with supermarket prices for produce, Mega Mandee would never have long lines at the cashier's. Instead, she focused on the exotic flowers she was smelling.

"And they keep all types of veggies. Zucchini, broccoli… celery too." The woman leaned in, as if to share a secret. "Free parking! Bombay totally needs more of these." She took the hand cream back. "So my driver today, he circles half an hour looking for a spot, and guess what, we still end up paying two hundred for street parking. Total madness. Easier to take a rickshaw, seriously." She zipped up her Prada.

"I took a rickshaw," Joohi said. "Got here so quickly." She did not reveal her promise to avoid the rickshaw for the next two weeks.

"Oh." The woman looked at Joohi, raising her eyebrows. Her gaze wandered from Joohi's silk stole to her feet, her half-chipped nail polish and worn-out leather sandal straps. She suppressed a smile. Joohi held her gaze over a lingering silence.

The girl in the white apron returned. Joohi excused herself and reclined into her chair. The girl poured a few drops of oil in her palm, rubbed her hands, and ran her fingers through Joohi's hair. She tapped on different points of Joohi's forehead. A laughing Buddha with a stuffed sack thrown across his shoulder and arms raised to the heavens hung on the wall across from them; his huge rosewood belly showcased a clock that ticked away. The Prada woman chitchatted with the girls giving her a pedicure, but Joohi tried to ignore all noise around her and inside her—the small talk, the tick-tock.

Take the girl out of Mount Sinai, but you can't take Mount Sinai out of the girl. Three children to take care of, Ram kasam.

Style queen once, Supperware agent now. And the Chinese empire as competition! The Almighty's mood swings, seriously yah.

She caressed the hem of her silk stole with the concentration of a yogi. She inhaled the jasmine-infused almond oil, relished the pressure of the girl's fingertips on her crown, her temples, her sinus points, and her nape. She felt the lines on her forehead dissolve. She closed her eyes, uncrossed her legs, and sank deep.

LADIES SPECIAL

As the ladies special fast train approaches Churchgate, the crowd moves closer to the edge of the platform. We move closer too. We align our bodies in the direction of the train's movement, sprint, and step inside before the dust-covered metallic beast trudges to a halt.

This is one of the first things you learn about taking a six p.m. ladies special. Climbing into a moving train—your only way to get a seat. We're pros, not a single sprain or fracture in the last fifteen years, not even in the monsoons.

Inside, I grab a window seat. Carol follows and slides toward me. Within seconds, all seats are taken.

Carol works at Deutsche Bank and walks to Churchgate Station every day. I'm a travel agent for Globetrotter at Marine Lines, the stop that comes after Churchgate, so I do the reverse journey first. I take a slow train to Churchgate, then catch the Virar fast that passes through Marine Lines without stopping there. This way, I'm almost sure to get a seat. And Carol's company over the long commute, our only downtime to share a heart-to-heart.

The extra commute gets on my nerves sometimes, especially in summer months when I'm doing double-duty ticketing at work, sending rich college kids backpacking in Europe, all eager to live their Bollywood adventure, get plastered, get laid. But then I remember Fatima, our other train buddy. "Would *kill* to have a seat for myself," she tells me often. "Tilt my head against the window and nap over commutes. I'd be so much more productive like that." Productive, that's her favorite word since she's started working at the American chain, Runway Shoes, in Dadar, a few stops north of Churchgate.

A desi-looking woman with blonde hair and Chinese eyes climbs into the train. She looks around and occupies the nook splitting the row of seats opposite us. Her head almost touches the metal rack where passengers have kept their handbags, raincoats, umbrellas, groceries. The blonde desi brings her henna-tattooed hands closer to her chest and starts reading a book. The cover displays a collage of images against a gray map of the city: Queen's Necklace bordering a little-too-blue Arabian Sea, an endless skyline with Ambani Residence highlighted in gold, the call centers at Bandra Kurla Complex, designer stores at Inorbit Mall and a group of half-naked women dancing against a Bollywood set. I lean forward, but don't see any of the guide names I know. No Lonely Planet logo either. The cover reads "Kazot Kreol" in one corner, maybe a tourist guide in a foreign language. "Mumbai" written in blood-red stands above the images.

By the time the train stops at Dadar, the compartment is so full, we wonder if Fatima will be able to climb in. We crane our necks toward the exit door. No sign of her.

The train moves again. The shrill of the metallic wheels blends with the drone of the fans on our compartment's ceiling. Rancid air adds to the stuffiness inside.

The women standing closer to the gate twitch; a couple of them scream at the fisherwoman who has sandwiched herself between two passengers. She forced her way forward while trying to balance a huge basket of fish on her head. Droplets of water trickle through.

"You're moving to the luggage compartment next stop or I'll call the police!" a woman yells as she brings her handkerchief to her nose.

"Train belong to your old man or what!" the fisherwoman squints.

More women grumble. Voices back and forth.

"The luggage compartment is full, can't you see?"

"The next train was to come in five minutes, couldn't you wait?"

"Why should *I* wait when none of you do?" the fisherwoman says.

"The stink from that water on my sari! Aiiyoooh, even Surf Ultra can't wash this away."

"Royalty should take first class then." The fisherwoman gives her basket a deliberate shake. The women around squeal and duck their heads.

I remove a cutting board from my bag and place it on my lap. "Drama every evening." I shake my head and start chopping carrots. A little kitchen work on the return commute goes a long way. I get done with dinner and cleaning at home earlier and can help my children with homework before bed. Productive, Fatima would say.

Carol returns fifty rupees in change to the aunty seated across from us. "I'll bring you the red ones tomorrow," she says as she offers Aunty a couple of yellow-and-green tiffin boxes. Aunty is Carol's regular customer for Supperware, a side business she runs over the train rides when she's not recruiting stay-at-home moms and single women as business partners, all hustling for a side income.

"Excuse me," a voice repeats in the distance, sounding more like *scuuz* me. Carol looks at me, a sparkle in her eyes. We love Fatima's town accent since she's started working at Runway. Fatima pushes through the crowd and plods toward us, panting for breath. We also love the fit-flop she wears these days with fake jadau buttons on the straps. Stylish yet functional, and the best part, Runway employees get a 75% discount. If only we had her shoe size.

Carol pushes her bag of Supperware products on the luggage rack above us. Fatima sits on her lap. We hi-hello, complain about the heat, catch up on our day, and vent about Wednesday, Sunday an eternity away. We fan ourselves, Fatima with the bottom of her tunic, Carol with a newspaper, and I, with my palm, every few seconds I stop chopping veggies.

"What news on the building, *babes?*" Fatima says, flashing her town vocabulary again. The girls know I was at my housing society's meeting yesterday. My building is to go for redevelopment like many others in our neighborhood. The three stories will be demolished and a twelve-story tower will be put up in their place. My family will get an extra room like other residents if we all accept the terms set in the construction contractor's agreement.

"Same old. The hag refuses to give in." I empty chopped carrots in a Supperware box to make room for radish. "Always one sample in the herd." The hag is my building's oldest resident, a widow unwilling to move and rent elsewhere for two years like the rest of us while the contractor builds a new tower.

Carol rubs my upper arm. The girls know how much I want the bigger space, especially with twins born to my brother. "A family of eight living in a one-bedroom flat—like being stuck in this fucking train compartment for good," I mutter, avoiding eye contact with the girls. Truth is, five years have passed with these meetings and I don't want to make-believe anymore, nod every time I share my building drama with them. Give it time, babes. What else will they say?

Our heads bob to the rhythm of the train's movement. Another train rushes past ours, the screech of its wheels drowning the chatter in our compartment. When the train disappears, glass-covered high-rises in the distance loom over three to four storied buildings like mine, where snakes of tar cover the outer walls to prevent monsoon water from leaking in. A long gutter separates Bombay from Mumbai.

"Aa." Carol pokes my knee. The women in our side of the compartment have started playing Antakshari. It's Carol's turn to sing a movie song beginning with A. *Ae dil hai mushkil jeena yahaan*, she begins, bringing her shoulder to pat mine. Fatima and Aunty join the singing, clapping hands in my direction. I force a smile and join the others.

Andheri approaches. Many get off, few climb in. Air at last.

Two women walk to our side of the compartment. One wears a black pencil skirt, a gray shirt, and a red scarf wrapped around her neck; another wears a blue shirtdress while her gelled hair is pulled back into a sleek ponytail. Both sport a badge on their arm that reads Voizone, Mumbai's biggest neighborhood for multinational call centers. They sit in the row next to ours. The desi blonde sits opposite them, the Mumbai guide still in her hands.

The sun sets outside. Sunrays light up the ads on the walls of our compartment: abortion ads, contraception ads, English-training and grooming-school ads, home-loan ads, and 919 helpline ads for police escorts women can call during late night and early morning commutes, a new service for passengers since the Delhi gang rape incident. An ad displaying Hindu divinity dominates the rest of the compartment walls. Under the entwined bodies of Shiva and Shakti dancing inside a circle of fire, the WhatsApp number of a gold-medalist Baba is listed. He assures a 100% wish fulfillment to your desires: white-collar job, good salary, fertility success, soulmate, cancer cure, migration abroad, American MBA, ration card, Green Card.

I'm singing with the girls *Yeh hai Bombay meri jaan* while chopping French beans on my lap. Below Baba's brochure, the desi blonde and Voizone women lean toward each other, chitchatting, laughing. The woman with the silk scarf points at something inside the firang's travel guide. The woman in the shirtdress types into her iPhone and nods at them. A Louis Vuitton knockoff hangs from her shoulder; the fingers tapping her iPhone sport French nails.

I stare at the dancing Shiva and Shakti who control the walls of our train, and give a shriek so loud that the chorus around me stops. I feel a sharp pain and put my finger in my mouth. Aunty gives a gasp and turns her head away. I look down at my cutting board and notice a sea of blood where chopped green beans have formed a pretty archipelago. Islands of different sizes have sprawled outward leaving a rectangular hollow in the center. This map reminds me of the shriveled back cover of an old guide on Bombay I've seen at Globetrotter's. Only senior employees can access the bookcase where the collector's copy stands tall, turning its back on us. As I taste the sweet sourness of my blood, I wonder what stories fill up the pages of the antique guide? Who plays the central character and who become footnotes in that fragmented city with a hollow center? What colors must the cover have used to name the ancient archipelago, bent on its refusal to cohere and bind? And what name?

TRADEOFF

"YOU NEED TO STOP being such a doormat," Dia said, as she removed the hip scarf covering her ankle-length skirt and put on a khadi jacket over her fitted block-printed tee. Watching her transformation from the dance rehearsal outfit into a desert gypsy, she searched for her older cousin in the mirror.

Joohi stayed silent at the other end of the room. Head bowed over a remote, she waved at the air conditioner's vent, making sure, perhaps, that it was working. It was early March, the beginning of summer, and Mumbai was already boiling.

"Today, women can have it all. Career, family, *love*—" Dia said, releasing her ponytail into naturally wavy hair and wrapping a batik bandana across her head. "What we need is to fuck the shit our mothers taught us—" She walked toward her cousin. "You know how good girls don't get a divorce, good girls don't get mad, good girls don't raise their voice, good girls blah blah." She eyed Joohi, wondering if she agreed.

Joohi kept nodding and putting clothes back on the display table. She'd saved money for months, spent hours convincing her in-laws, run endless errands in Mumbai's heat to rent the exhibition hall for a day in Upper Worli, for Joohi Mittal's first sale of personally designed clothes.

"No, really." Dia glided toward the display table. Standing opposite her cousin, chin held high—first lesson learned in dance class—she was determined not to play the diplomat. Today might be their last one-on-one meeting before she migrated to Chicago for grad school with Aziz. She'd been saving up for her American dream for years too, while recovering from substance abuse and waiting for Aziz to return from his job in the Philippines. And now, she was leaving behind family, friends, Mumbai, and a job offer from a top-notch Bollywood choreographer to begin a new life oceans away. To Joohi, Dia might be a twenty-something idealist but of all the Mittal women, she knew the cost of choosing freedom. Didn't she?

Dia's cellphone vibrated. Aziz's name flashed across the screen with a picture of two interlocked hands. She ignored the call, knowing it was a reminder to finish applications for campus jobs that would cover their MBA tuition in the U.S.

"After all, the man cheated on you!" Dia said, spacing out kurtis and leheria skirts on the rack. Divorce is what she wanted to suggest again but she resisted. "Besides, that hypochondriac mother of his. She has rarely seen a daughter-in-law in you. Only a free maid."

"Dia darling," Joohi said. "Wait till you're older and have children." She rearranged mojaris that clients had left scattered on the shoe rack. "Love turns into something bigger than a romcom script." She looked up at Dia.

Dia smirked. Typical of Joohi to insinuate how Dia was running away with her boyfriend for a Hollywood fantasy instead of confronting what she really wanted.

"But that man and his mother—they don't deserve you!"

"I know." Joohi sighed, looping an orange-and-pink stole around her neck. "But the kids deserve better. An emotional anchor, a stable home to grow up in," she said. "Their dad's death, the move to Malava, and now, a new father, new home, new school, new friends. It hasn't been easy for them."

The cousins had been through this a few times already. Dia knew Joohi's commitment to her kids. And Joohi knew how much Dia disliked her new husband.

"And you? What's *your* emotional anchor?" Dia asked.

"This." Joohi raised her chin, surveying the clothes on display from left to right, an explosion of hot colors—turmeric, yellow, orange, rani pink, maroon, red. She pulled a striped lehenga to expose its massive flare bordered by intricate mirrorwork. "Traditionally, the number of pleats in a skirt was a measure of prosperity," she said. "This one's a hundred pleats, and about six months of manual labor."

Last year, for her college's annual day performance, Dia had worn a skirt of eighty pleats designed by Joohi for which she received rave reviews, in addition to her dancing. Dia had always marveled at her cousin's skill at coordinating colors, fabrics, textures, and silhouettes; still, so many hours spent on one skirt? Wow.

"And this." Joohi returned to the shoe rack. "In old days, these were made for North Indian royalty," she said, running her fingers over a mojari's colorful embroidery. "Embroidered with real silver and gold threads."

Dia followed Joohi who moved toward tie-dye sarongs, bandhani scarves, and blockprinted stoles. Her older cousin shared the history and labor behind each item on display. She catalogued the ways in which she imported a Rajasthani legacy into urban fashion—the power of a bandhani scarf, for instance, to create radically different looks, from conservative office wear to desi boho.

Joohi turned to the section for trousers. "Jodhpurs are my favorite," she said, pulling out a pair of chrome-yellow pants, baggy on the thighs and tapering at the ankles. "So much more personality and freedom for movement than the good ol' saree. If I were living alone, I'd never slip out of these." She stroked the finely embroidered peacocks sitting on the side pockets.

Dia's phone buzzed. A text message popped on the screen. "Job apps due on Monday! Me here. Where's you?" Yikes. She forgot she was supposed to meet Aziz at four.

"Jodhpurs stole the show at the Turf Club Fashion Gala last month," a voice spoke from behind the cousins. They turned around to see a middle-aged man in linen pants and a beige shirt that highlighted cinnamon strands in his grey hair.

"Welcome, Sir," Joohi said.

The man gave a slight nod. "Manish Mehra closed his collection wearing jodhpurs on the ramp too. A-list Bollywood is still debating if it was a style hit or a royal miss."

"Equestrian fashion was the gala's theme," Joohi said with a certain nonchalance. "Jodhpurs weren't a bad move."

"Agree." The man put out a hand. "J.J. Kejriwal."

Dia discreetly checked him out. *JJK*. Didn't think one of the most revered names in Indian fashion would look this young, and this good.

"Oh," Joohi said. "I loved your latest office wear inspired by Buddhist cave paintings." Chin high, shoulders thrown back; her voice was assured. "Chiffon shirts in earthy tones self-printed with mural art. Flamboyant, yet professional."

Playing with scarves at a distance, Dia listened while Joohi complimented the style mogul's impact on desi fashion, his clever weaving of function with form.

"Our winter collection is inspired by the Silk Road." JJK handed her his business card. "Let's see more of your desert-inspired work?"

"It would be an honor, Sir," Joohi said, voice lowered.

Dia could bet what her cousin was thinking. Hubby and mamma-in-law. Who'd convince them to let Joohi off the leash? After all, design as a housewifely hobby was one thing, design as a professional pursuit, another. Working in Mumbai's leading design studio? Mingling with male colleagues, models, Bollywood actors—an open call to corruption.

Dia's phone buzzed. A second text. Craigslist in Chicago had awesome deals on used furniture. Seventy dollars only for the desk-and-futon combo they'd liked at IKEA.com.

Dia looked at her watch. Three-forty.

"A twenty-hour workweek max," Joohi said.

"Sure, let's work something out," JJK said, browsing through her creation by the office wear section. "What I want in my clothes is a presence of Shekhawati havelis."

Joohi told JJK about *Style* magazine's latest issue on Rajasthani women, the sartorial paintings on Marwari havelis and their avant-garde transnational style. JJK kept nodding, seemingly agreeing with every word. What camaraderie between the two, what synergy in the room.

As the duo talked, Dia remembered the rehearsal for her college's annual day performance. Undulating her torso as if riding the waves of the Arabian Sea, she demonstrated a belly roll to the girls in her troupe. She locked eyes with them before twirling together to an A.R. Rahman song. What camaraderie between them, what synergy in the room.

Joohi and JJK were now talking about the Thar Desert and its textile influence on Bollywood blockbusters, including *Rasleela*, Filmfare's latest winner for costume design. As she followed the carefree sway of Joohi's arms, the glint in her eyes, the authority in her voice, she felt the rhythm of her breathing accelerate. A strange sensation tickled her torso, gooseflesh overtook her body. Her phone buzzed again.

Years would pass before Dia would recall a synergy that had filled up auditoriums too, a carefree sway with which she moved to percussion beats on the stage to the applause of a few thousand hands seated below. Years would pass before she'd stop switching homes, jobs, and love interests to consider what her body was trying to tell her that moment, what she'd repeatedly dismissed in her Voizone years as new-agey Californian crap she'd learned as a call-center agent serving Americans—that Om Shanti Shanti BS, vocation, life force, chi, even dharma, or that which upholds you, as her Yoga instructor would remind her in a life years later on the other side of the planet, *in* California.

Overhearing her cousin that afternoon though, Dia told herself what she'd been telling herself throughout her Mumbai years, that real freedom involved the use of free will in forging one's path—a rational, proactive, masculine approach to life.

Her phone buzzed again. As she took the screeching device in her hands, she glanced at her cousin for the last time and rushed toward the exit.

9/12

THEY SAT OUTSIDE IN Janpada's only bar, a dimly lit room with stained walls and a patio of sorts holding two plastic tables and a few chairs. Mumbai elections were around the corner as was Ganesh Chaturthi, celebrating the divine slayer of obstacles for eleven days over free meals and megahit Bollywood numbers. To them, this meant one thing: a bomb could explode anytime, anywhere in their neighborhood, triggering communal violence and replacing one political leader with another.

After the terrorist attacks in September 2015 at one of the city's biggest luxury hotels, The Raj Mahal was renovated and remarketed to its multinational clientele. Sonu, Yadav, Abdul and Francis were part of the hotel's new staff, although this did not prevent them from recycling stories about the attacks they'd heard from the older employees.

"A firangi couple tried to escape by tying bed sheets to their room's window," Sonu said, helping himself to desi daru. "The man fell on his way down to the street and got paralyzed. The couple sued Raj for ten crores!" Sonu worked as a gardener at The Raj Mahal.

"Sisterfuckers! If we fell from the window and got paralyzed, would they give us money?" Yadav spat on the muddy floor where a jug was tossed away, empty of the cheap country liquor Bar Fancy specialized in. "Everything in this country, everything everywhere sucks up to white skin." He slapped his arm and killed a mosquito. He worked as The Raj Mahal's watchman from six in the morning to ten in the evening.

"Not true, mian," Abdul, the cook, said. "There were many foreigners in the wedding party my senior was serving. The terrorists asked only for those with American and British passports. The Italian there got spared."

"British or American, tell you, man, no one more precious than Jews," Francis, the janitor, said. "If they had Jews by the balls, they would release every other gora ass."

"True," Sonu said.

"Anything done to Jews and America would not spare Pakistan," Abdul said.

"Anything done to Jews and America would not spare *any* country," Francis said. They raised their glasses to touch each other's.

Every time Janpada geared up for a national holiday or a religious festival, their recollection about the 2015 attacks got longer and louder. Across the open sewer running next to the bar, two men were erecting a wooden stage for a gigantic idol of Ganesha to be worshipped in public first by Janpada's ruling politician; he would arrive the following day in a bulletproof saffron limo with his crew of bodyguards.

"I've to say—" Sonu closed his eyes, as if focusing hard to sit still. "A Jewish tourist helped children get out first. I saw his photo in the newspaper a few days later."

"One Jew! What about the hotel staff, cooks, bellboys, janitors? What of that, boss? They helped the wedding guests, NRIs, goras, women and children get out first." Francis cringed at the click of a camera. "You saw any of their photos in a newspaper?" He pulled his chair closer to his friends to avoid looking at a white woman photographing them from a distance. Next to the stage for Ganesha stood a deluxe bus with GoLoco Travels written across its body.

He couldn't stand goras visiting Janpada in growing numbers after the success of some Hollywood movie showcasing life in Mumbai slums. At least the goras at the Raj were there for a reason: a wedding, a business meeting, or just to enjoy the food. They did not gape at him and his buddies as if they were circus dogs.

"Life and death not in hands of God, bhai, not a question of skin color or country. All about who has what in bank." Yadav rubbed Francis's shoulder; he understood his friend's irritation. "One who escapes death is the one with most moolah."

"Or luck. A bullet hit one cook's leg and got blocked by the beer-bottle opener in his pocket," Abdul said.

"One gora jumped from his window to escape and died, while two motherfuckers waiting in their room got rescued."

"Life or death in whose hands, mian?"

"True, true." They shook their head sideways.

"Raj managers paid families of cooks and janitors five lakh rupees each. If I'd known, I'd die just for the money," Yadav said.

"Smart move that would be, sisterfucker. In a city like this, how long would five lakhs last?"

"Five lakhs, ladies and gents. Our price if we die saving hotel guests one day."

"Three hundred died that day."

"More like five hundred plus. News reporters, sons of whores, always reducing the number by half."

"And four cooks helping others were Muslim. But no mention of them anywhere. I mean, think about it—" Abdul poured more daru in his glass. "We Muslims, always the media's bitch, the white man's bitch, America's bitch—"

"Array, who's media's bitch depends on who's ruling this country—"

They continued their stories while other men filled up tables at the bar—construction workers, taxi and rickshaw drivers, fishermen, street hawkers, all wrapping up their week, hoping for a break from the September heat, from the soreness in their muscles. Some would pass out by their tables, others would visit a brothel, and yet others would go home and beat their wives.

One man looked at his watch and yelled at the ten-year-old waiter to switch the channel on the box television balanced precariously over a stool inside. "Bomb threat at City Central station today, motherfucker," the man said.

The fisherwoman with a sheer saree bellyrolling amid drunken men on the TV screen gave way to news images where a plane flying into a skyscraper alternated with people of different colors facing the camera, and repeating with pride, "I'm an American." Bar Fancy was transitioning into a new day, but somewhere far away, time ran slow.

ANCHOR

THE PLANE HOVERED OVER Mumbai's international airport, slammed by monsoon winds. Dia ignored the nausea rising from her belly and looked out of her window. A bluish-black Arabian Sea bordered the sprawling carpet of lights.

"I want you to forget this city," her widowed mother had told her. "I want you to create new memories, and stories other than the survival game."

"I'll create new memories for both of us, Ma," Dia had said. "I promise."

The crew captain's voice blared on the intercom. "We hope to begin our descent in fifteen minutes. Please keep your seat-belts fastened." The plane had been circling over the city for about an hour.

On hearing the announcement, passengers fidgeted in their seats. Sixteen hours of flight nonstop from Newark to Mumbai, not counting the bus ride from D.C. to Newark.

Dia's neighbor resumed their conversation. "So many senior executives travel first class on company expense," she said. "I hear American MNCs pay really well."

"They're not bad, Aunty." Dia straightened her back, sore from her last evening in D.C. She had typed nonstop for fourteen hours, finishing her annual performance reports, her final responsibility as senior analyst with Goldman's before leaving on a sabbatical she'd managed to negotiate. She didn't tell them she might never return.

"Chalo, few minutes more, one-year vacation then. Your family will pamper you so much. When my son visits from Toronto, we do same. You'll see."

"I hope so, Aunty." Dia forced a smile, not sharing her apprehensions. She folded the fellowship offer in her hand from Melbourne Institute of Arts, one she kept rereading, and put it back into her purse. Of course her family would pamper her. She hadn't been home for four years.

"Besides, you could easily meet someone. One year is a long time. My son met his wife in Bombay too. Before, they met on Shaadi.com. These days, with internet, marriage so easy."

Dia nodded at the seat rows ahead. A pair of long arms stretched in the air, above a head full of gelled black curls. On the sleeve of an orange sweatshirt, Caltech printed in white.

"Even in Bombay these days, people getting married late. Women want to work, like you. Job first, marry later."

"I'm hardly ready for marriage, Aunty."

"Why? Twenty-eight, not that late. Your family must worry about you."

Dia tapped her fingers on the seat ahead, one of them bruised from removing Pete's too-tight engagement ring. "Just not…the right time."

The crew captain requested the passengers to switch off their electronic devices. A runway had opened up and they were to descend. Aunty and the rest of the passengers began clapping. Dia joined them too, craving pav bhaji with chilled masala lemonade the way Ma made it.

Dia followed the passengers past the long corridor. Her muscles loosened up and her swollen feet didn't hurt as much. When she reached the immigration counters, the line had turned around, zigzagged a few times, and she found herself waiting at the end of a mob. This crowded an airport at three in the morning?

The rise in the room temperature felt sudden and strong. Dia took off her cardigan. She noticed her flight neighbor in the line staring at the edge of her tank top, tight-lipped. Dia looked at her shoulder. Her purple bra strap peeped out. She nodded at Aunty.

The guy ahead of Dia, the one seated in the plane's front row, was taking off his orange hoodie.

"Did you enjoy L.A.?" she asked him, her chin pointing to the Caltech written across his sweatshirt.

"Loved it." He turned around. "Amazing how the weather spoils you. Better get out before the sun lassos you for good, right?"

"What brings you to Mumbai?" She tried to place his hybrid accent. He looked Indian but wasn't. Not American either.

"New job. And wanderlust, you can say."

"L.A. to Mumbai. That's quite a switch."

His shoulders rose and fell. "It's only for a year."

As they moved forward in the line, Dia learned that this was his first time in Mumbai, home city to his parents until they moved to Lagos, and then to Leicester. He'd always wanted to visit Mumbai and work had finally brought him here.

"What brings you back?" he said.

"Want to belong somewhere." She tousled her hair. "Living out of boxes starts getting old."

He smiled. "Return to roots?"

"Some would say."

The guy looked at Dia as if waiting to hear more. Dia found herself opening up. She worried about her family's reaction were she to give up her senior position at Goldman's and start over in Australia and the arts, at twenty-eight, an age to settle down, not to start all over again, not in the arts, and certainly not in a new country as a single woman. Wasn't it time she supported her widowed mother? her uncles and aunts would say.

"You should've heard my old man on this move to India." The Caltech guy shared his family's frustration when he decided to move again *at the peak of his career.* "That dharma shit is overrated, you know? Or maybe just misunderstood." He held her gaze. "Cuz at the end of the day, if you choose duty over joy, you lose big."

When he picked up his bag and moved toward the lady at the immigration desk, Dia sensed that he wanted to continue the conversation. She waved goodbye, resisting her desire to ask his name. Aziz, Danny, Francisco, Pete, she was done with men.

When she stepped forward for her turn, the lady behind the immigration counter neither looked at her nor smiled. The lady reached for the passport, flipped a few pages, stamped the right one, and threw it back on the desk. Dia thanked her; the lady raised her arm to summon the next passenger.

At the conveyer belt, Dia saw a red Samsonite moving toward her. She sandwiched herself between two families and pulled the suitcase off. A short, skinny guy came over, asked if she needed help with her bag, then moved on to other foreigners.

Dia followed the exit sign. Amazing how much the airport had changed. Duty-free shops, new food court with American chains like Panda Express, Chipotle, and Indian fast food. Billboards for Absolut Vodka and MacBook Air hung above the arrival hall. A lady at a kiosk asked, "Exchange currency, Ma'am?" Another guy came over and asked, "Taxi, Madam?"

Why were they asking her? This was her country and Ma was coming to pick her up in Cool Cab. Couldn't they see her? Brown skin, black eyes, black hair. As she kept walking, she overheard a man talking on his cell phone about the bland food on the flight. Maha pakau, yaar, he said. She chuckled at the Bombay lingo she hadn't heard in ages.

When she stepped into the arrival hall, a wave of heat slammed her. A mob grew in size, held back by a frail iron railing. Wow, we're that many? This short and skinny too? She tugged her hair into a ponytail to air out her neck. She noticed people from behind the railing staring at her. She pushed her bra strap inside her tank top. She'd gotten used to D.C.'s muggy summers but this early monsoon humidity felt so much heavier. She looked up and noticed a foggy sky—neither dark nor bright, just a steady gray hiding the stars. Sweat trickled under her tank top; she pulled her top back and forth to relieve herself. She sniffed the foul air around her for traces of fresh oxygen. As she searched for Ma in the tsunami of people restrained by a railing, she found them staring back at her. Their eyes, dark and still, mirrored her own look of confusion, irritation and disdain.

CHUTNEY

DIA AND HER DATE, Yash, stood clapping with the crowd at the end of the performance. Two comedians bowed on the stage ahead: one desi, born and raised in Mumbai; another, desi American, fresh off the flight from New Jersey. Throughout their playoff, the comic duo had dissed each other. Dia and Yash had laughed at the same jokes on Bollywood, Apu, chai tea latte, Hot Yoga and haggling on Fashion Street, but were they laughing with the same jokes, she wondered as they walked to the food court in Archipelago, a new megamall built in one of Mumbai's defunct cotton mills. Around her were young professionals in weekend mode: women in jodhpurs and spaghetti tops, bandhani kurtis and capris, linen palazzos and tees with mojaris; men in blockprinted shorts, fitted shirts, ear studs, ponytails, or goatees, flip-flops too. Here, no overload of Guccis, Louis Vuittons, and Ferragamos she'd seen in Phoenix Mills over her first date with Yash. In this commercial complex of seven high-rises connected by manmade canals to honor the city's past, in this Mumbai bringing together the old and the new, the rooted and the uprooted, she could reintegrate, she thought.

"Sushi at Zen?" Yash asked as they reached the elevators, pointing to the bistro upstairs, sandwiched between Brooklyn Pizza and Tandoor Nation.

"Prawn kathi roll?" She looked at the colorful food carts on the street below. Chaat Express, Masala Corn Company, Wrap & Roll.

"You want a *roti*?" he asked. "Zen here is competing with the Morimotos of the world, dude."

"Sushi is not what I missed in the U.S., *dude*," she said. "Desi spiced prawns though—" She licked her lips.

"Looks like someone didn't convert after all?" Yash knew about the American cities she'd lived in. Family grapevine, naturally.

"And someone did—headlong," she said. Yash had just returned home after finishing an MBA at Kellogg.

"How about takeout and meet at the food court?" Yash flapped open his wallet. "Our usual spot?"

"Yes, Sir." She took the elevator going down.

Standing outside her mother's flat in Gorgao where she was temporarily living, Dia straightened her tee and removed what remained of her lipstick. She folded the Kleenex and wiped her lips a second time, hard. She rang the doorbell.

"Back early, *again*." Ma opened the door and jutted her head out. "He couldn't come up to say hello?"

Dia took off her sandals, avoiding eye contact. "He has to work early tomorrow."

Ma sauntered back to the sofa in their living room. Stacks of mint and cilantro and two Supperware boxes sat on the coffee table. She resumed her chore, snipping leaves off their stems to make her green chutney, known in all of their family for its inimitable flavor. The television was on.

Dia sank into the divan across from the sofa. A bunch of clothes lay strewn there, taken off the strings outside the balcony where Ma hung them routinely to dry. A birdcage tinkled in the background. In the window next to their balcony, their neighbor's pet, a lovebird called Nargis, stood against the gray of Mumbai's smoggy sky.

Dia folded a batik salwaar into four. "You had a good day?"

She broke Ma's palpable silence.

"Not bad." Ma twisted a cilantro bunch to separate the leaves from the stems. She complained that the electrician hadn't come to fix the air conditioner but the plumber fixed the shower. She'd gotten fresh vegetables for half the price from the neighborhood market and guess who stopped by to deliver a wedding invitation. Runa Aunty. Sonam, her daughter, was getting married at forty. Finally!

Dia ignored Ma's tone as if Sonam's late wedding was her fault. "Archipelago was fun," she said. "Love their art galleries, the indie theater, and oh, the food—" she told Ma about the kathi roll, prawns with the smoky flavor of a real tandoor she missed so much in the U.S. "Only thing was the chutney. Too gora in taste. Like a single flavor of puréed mint." She moved a pile of linen pants to make room for another pile. "I mean, the whole point of chutney is to blend flavors, no? Mint, cilantro, peanuts, cumin seeds, lemon, and all that good stuff...just like you do." She looked up, hoping for a moment of recognition from Ma that after all these years abroad, she hadn't forgotten her cooking.

Ma kept snipping leaves off herb stems and placing them into a Supperware.

"Clearly, we're all becoming confused desis," Dia chuckled, wondering if Ma understood.

"Tell me you're not moving again." Ma cut through her monologue, waving the Australian job offer Dia had hidden under her bed. "I thought we were done with this."

A high-pitched wail emanated from the TV screen. Tulsi, the queen of Zee TV soap operas, cried in front of her parents-in-law. The camera zoomed in and out of her heavily kajaled eyes.

"It's a sweet deal," Dia said, hiding her irritation at Ma's violation of her privacy.

Dia had planned to return to this conversation once they had Yash out of the picture. "The best part? People from all over the world live in Melbourne, and so many of Indian descent." She had practiced this pitch to herself a couple of times already, as if the prospects of a desi husband would make Ma open to Dia switching homes and careers again—a two-year fellowship in Australia to research desert arts across the world, including Marwari dances and haveli paintings.

Ma knew how much Dia loved dancing and arty "hobbies" in general: painting, theater, movies, writing. She also knew her daughter longed for a break from her life as a corporate consultant and from living out of boxes in the U.S. She snapped mint leaves off their twigs and threw them into a Supperware. A few scattered on the coffee table.

"Not made a decision yet," Dia said, knowing how much her mother wanted her to settle down, take root somewhere, starting with a man. "I mean, I'll always have you and the motherland but to be home—" She looked over their balcony window. Nargis jerked her neon-green wings. Their neighbor's pet was restless by nature, always flapping her wings as if ready to fly out of her cage. Maybe Nargis missed being at home too.

"You *have* made a decision. You *are* staying back." Ma walked to the switchboard next to the TV and turned up the fan. "Once married, you and Yash are free to go wherever you want—together." She returned to her sofa and tossed the Australian offer into a Supperware with herb twigs waiting to be trashed.

"Me and Yash?" Dia asked.

"You and Yash."

"Why Yash?"

"Why not Yash?"

"Maybe because we want different things?"

"Which two people ever want the same things?"

Dia plucked at the neck of her shirt to fan herself. "Chemistry is so important, Ma," she returned to her former spiel on Yash, her doubts on settling back in Mumbai for good too.

"Your uncles, aunties, cousins, we're all waiting for you to settle down. We've let you date, study abroad, travel the world, and now that you've returned, this perfect guy comes along, and you're back to your antics." Ma crossed her legs in Sukhasana, a sign she was only getting started. "Queen Jodha will say yes to no one short of Emperor Akbar. Such larger-than-life stories you girls have these days, head full of fantasies you pick up from Hollywood, Bollywood, and oh, what's that word? Passion!"

"I want to settle down too, take root *somewhere*." Dia folded a pair of jeans. "Life is short for compromise, though. When the right man comes along, I'll settle."

Nargis chirped and straightened her vermilion neck. Dia couldn't help smiling at the reputedly monogamous baby parrot. Nargis and she, didn't they belong to the same race? Lovebirds filled with desire for the one—the right partner, the right home.

"All these years we listened to you, this time, you're listening to us," Ma said. "Enough time we've given you to gallivant across the city without getting engaged. Yash likes you, his family loves you. We love Yash. This time, you're making the right decision." She lurched her head forward, making clear that by the right decision, she meant family consensus on their latest joint venture in matchmaking.

"What about what *I* like?"

"At least you can acknowledge a family that shows interest on their own, not minding our middle-class status at all."

"Actually, my MBA and American jobs make up for our bank balance in a desi checklist for trophy wife."

"As if five years of life abroad has washed away desi genes from your blood. Better than Surf Ultra!"

"Mother. I listened to you, I went out with Yash, I gave us another try." Dia dried her sweaty neck with the back of her wrist. Damn the broken air conditioner. Three calls to the electrician in the last five days and still no show. "I can't marry this guy." She tried not to think of Yash's tongue down her throat in the car earlier that evening, and how she wanted to push him away. So attentive to performance, his stiff grip on her waist, his hands racing to her breasts, as if on a timer to prove his sexual prowess. With Yash, it was all about proving. His Ferragamo belt, his BMW, his

Kellogg degree, the apartment he was hunting at The Parthenon in Upper Worli, Mumbai's latest hub for expats.

"Eight meetings and you've made a decision! Besides, who's perfect? You tell me. Your uncle's best friend's sister's family knows Yash, their family is modern, he wants a working girl, and you want an educated boy. Senior post at Mahindra's, not bad to look at, and your reason to reject him, that silly idea again—chemistry." Ma continued churning out classic lines on the wisdom of arranged marriages in India, the failure of love marriages in the U.S., a Mammasutra of sorts every woman in their extended family had heard at some point, from her mother, from other mothers.

Dia kept folding clothes, resisting the urge to remind Ma that her own arranged marriage wasn't a resounding success. Alongside Ma's harangue, Tulsi moaned on Zee TV. Dia blinked, wondering if desi soap operas borrowed from reality or created it.

"I'm only twenty-eight, Ma. A two-year gig is perfect timing for soul-searching now that I've savings to afford the luxury." She raised a pair of pants to release its wrinkles. "Can you please understand?"

"Understand what? You think your father and I felt chemistry when we were married? We slept in separate beds for the first three months! Attraction develops when you get to know someone over time. Not everything in life comes instant like in the U.S., microwaveable!"

Dia rubbed her toes against the floor's brown tiles meant to resemble hardwood flooring. "Working on chemistry ain't my style, Mother." She explained her take on chemistry, that mysterious pull between two people that was either there or made itself visible pretty early in the game.

Ma narrowed her eyes as if considering. Dia reminded her how generous the fellowship stipend was, how she could fly home often from Melbourne and see if settling back in Mumbai was truly for her. Besides, Melbourne was so diverse, maybe Mr. Right was there, waiting?

"Every time you move to a new city, I worry about you." Ma said, choking up. "Once you've a partner to lean on, I'll be tension-free, settle down in my own life. I'm sixty-one and still working fifty hours a week, saving all these years for your wedding." Across from their living room, Nargis nodded, as if rooting for Ma in their predictable mother-daughter tragicomedy.

A BEST bus grunted on the street. The rickshaws and cars honked. Dia tried not to think of Ma's four-hour commute, first by auto, then a bus, then a train, commute she'd been doing for thirty years to her job as an accountant at Deutsche Bank. The guilt alone would make her settle for Yash and Mumbai. Ma was saving up for a grand desi wedding should the groom's family want it, a grand wedding Dia refused to have.

"Would love to support you," Dia said. "Student loans finally paid off. With the fellowship, it'll *finally* be possible."

"You could have a good job here too, were the thrill of adventure not lurking around." Ma shrugged. "You mark my words, child. If you refuse this man, you are going to remain single for the rest of your life!" She moved on to her aching knees, the importance of seizing opportunities at the right time, the willingness to gamble in marriage. That her own marriage was a steep gamble never seemed to make her question her spiel.

Nargis chirped louder and synced to Ma's aria. Tulsi on Zee TV played stoic and wiped her tears at her son's birthday party. As Dia watched the tragedy queen lower a toddler over a blue cake in the shape of a heart, a memory she'd often had since migrating to the U.S. returned. She was cutting a carrot-halwa cake Ma had made for her sixth birthday. She remembered the excitement she felt blowing off the candles over an orange heart made for her alone as her parents sang to her. Ma and Papa would also beat her up each time they fought in their former flat in Bombay. Once, around the same age, Papa had knocked Dia's head against the wall after one of those epic fights with Ma. Yet each time she thought of her family abroad, the orange heart crossed her mind first, seldom the red of her bleeding head. And now that a few years had passed since Papa's death from cancer, Ma herself seemed to remember only the sunny side of her marriage. Dia rubbed her toes against their faux-wood floor again. Strange detergent, nostalgia—purifies the past like nothing else. Better than Surf Ultra.

Ma returned to the topic of Sonam who'd dated men for twenty years and was finally saying yes to an arranged marriage. How happy Sonam was with her fiancé now; she was completely unattracted to him when they first met. How important it was in life to take chances, to be open to new possibilities, to let go of perfectionism, to…to…to.

Hearing Ma drag her mamalogue on marriage, Dia felt a bizarre tickling chafe her belly. Sweat bordered her lips; her head began to pound. And she couldn't tell what it was: Tulsi playing the sacrificial lamb on TV, the rickshaws honking below, Nargis's frantic chirping, or the reminder of violence our deepest love can hold.

"Will you shut up, bitch?" Dia stood up. "SHUT. UP. PUHLEEEASE. You're fucking suffocating me."

Pin-drop silence. Ma switched off the TV. On the other side of the room, Nargis stopped moving her wings.

For the first time, Dia had cussed at Ma whom she loved more than anyone in the world, Ma whom she missed when lonely or heartbroken in the U.S. As the duo stared at each other, a birdcage in the background stopped moving. And it dawned on Dia. If she opened the cage, Nargis, nervous, constantly fluttering her wings, would not fly out into the city. How often had their neighbor kept the cage open while feeding seeds to his pet? Nargis flapped her wings because the cage was too small, and Mumbai's sensorial overload too much. Not enough though to force her into risking the unknown. In the city's homicidal heat, smog, and din, Nargis had reinvented home. In the island of her cage, the lovebird had taken root, committed to the flavor of a single place. Nargis belonged to the race of settlers. And Dia, hereafter, to the race of wanderers.

EXCURSION

MADAM WAS OUTSIDE IN her air-conditioned hall, holding court again with her new best friends. Sir, her husband, was out for work, as always, and her two sons were away at boarding school in Shimla. That didn't stop her from spoiling her niece, Sweetie Di, and Sweetie Di's fiancé, Amrikan Sir. They lived in Amrika and had come to Mumbai to officially get married, a month in advance of their wedding date. Their families were to fly here a week before the wedding. Meanwhile, Madam was in charge of the wedding preparations, including Sweetie Di's wardrobe.

"This is my chance to spoil a daughter," Madam told Sweetie Di when I went out to serve them fresh sweet lime juice. This, after the fresh coconut water I'd served them half an hour back when they'd gotten here.

Madam tied the knot of a heavily embroidered blouse Di had put on. "How you girls can be so skinny!" she told Di, the same way she would tell her boys each time they returned from Shimla. "A month of real desi food will add flesh to these bones." She pulled the blouse up so the collar rested on Di's small shoulders. "Look at these mosquito bites—" She almost squeezed Di's breasts and pulled back the blouse to tighten her waistline. "No good for marriage."

"Masi, *please*." Di recoiled, blushing.

I put the juice glasses down on the coffee table. Amrikan Sir was sitting on the sofa, watching TV and sipping his whiskey. I picked up the bowls with dry fruit leftovers, returned to the kitchen, and shut the glass door as Madam had strictly told me to. The heat inside rushed toward me like the Ladies Special fast train. I opened the oven, placed the tray full of baatis inside, and adjusted the temperature to 400 degrees. I turned up the gas flame and scattered chopped onions into the frying pan. They hissed and crackled in the sunflower oil.

Dry fruit, paneer-stuffed baatis, dal made of five different types of lentils, ker saangar, mango rabdi, and malai lassi. Only rich fuckers can digest that kind of food in May. Shut in their air-conditioned rooms, air-conditioned cars, air-conditioned malls, they can down beef korma and fried puris and still not complain of heavy food. But if they had to step outside and breathe natural air, or Goddess forbid, drink unbottled water? Nothing then could stop them from hitting the grave.

As I stirred the onions, my eyes watered again. And I didn't know what it was. The fatigue, the insomnia, or the homicidal heat in the kitchen. All I knew was I missed Josna and Yadav. It had been a week since I had a word from Josna, the maid who used to live in the kitchen with me, the only friend I had since I moved to Mumbai, the carefree teenager who could afford quitting. The moment Madam found out about Josna, she took my pair of flat keys so I wouldn't attempt running away too. It had also been a week since I'd spoken to Yadav, the watchman who guarded the building across from us, the only man I'd come close to calling what they say in movies: a boyfriend.

"Shalu!" a voice rose outside. Reflexively, I took the duster in my hand, wiped the sweat dripping from my forehead, and rushed out.

"How often have I told you to wipe the dust off each leaf?" Madam said, pointing to the money plant with giant leaves in a corner of the hall. Sweetie Di and Amrikan Sir were to visit again that evening with a famous designer, some guy called JJK, and try more wedding clothes.

I nodded. I kneeled. I wiped *each* leaf of the money plant again. I didn't tell Madam that I'd already wiped the leaves in the morning when she and Sir were sleeping in the bedroom and the hall windows were open. With Mumbai's pollution, it wasn't my fault.

If only I didn't need the cash tips from Sweetie Di's wedding to send to my family. Papa was getting knee replacement surgery in Kathmandu, hours away from our village in Nepal. Even if they were to use their savings of the last two decades, it wouldn't cover a third of the surgery cost. *Nothing* in our village paid the way Mumbai did.

I took the third round of refreshments for the firangis. "Fresh pineapple juice and rasmalai, Madam," I told Sweetie Di as she chit-chatted with Madam.

"Call me Di," she said. I nodded as I put rasmalai bowls on the coffee table. Her legs were as fair as Kareena Kapoor's. Everyone goes to Amrika and becomes really fair, Yadav had said when we grocery-shopped together and I'd told him about Madam's foreign family who looked like goras. At The Raj Mahal, firangi desis were everywhere; he told me about the job he had at one of Mumbai's luxury hotels before becoming watchman for our residential complex. That was the day before Josna left, and I didn't know then that it would be our last outdoor meeting too, Yadav and mine. I returned to the kitchen and checked the minutes left on my phone, few and for emergencies only. I resisted the urge to text Yadav. My folks had called me from Nepal again. They were desperate, and I needed to save up on the phone bills.

"Shaluuuuuu." Thunder struck in the hall again. I slid my phone under the blanket in the kitchen corner where I slept. I straightened my dupatta, put cucumber pakoras on a serving tray, and stepped out into the hall's Himalayan air.

"Om Shanti Shanti, Masi." Amrikan Sir was swaying his palm up and down in slow motion. "With your voice, you could replace that Modi dude in elections," he said, ogling Di who was wearing a new lehenga studded with crystals and a backless choli embroidered with silver. Instead of telling him to get some shame, Madam picked up a pakora from my tray.

"Try these, Babu," she said, placing it between his lips. "They're fresh." She then turned toward me, blood in her eyes. "How many times have I told you to serve piping hot pakoras?" She oscillated her palm between Amrikan Sir and Di. "Like these two visit us everyday!"

I slid the leftover pakoras from their plate on the table onto my serving tray with a pair of tongs. Madam would lose it again if she saw me touch the food with my fingers, especially in front of her firangi family. My hands trembled and a few fell on the floor.

"No matter how much you teach these girls, they just don't get it," Madam told Di as I replaced the hotter pakoras on their plate.

Di tapped Madam's shoulder. "Why waste, Masi? With AC, these won't stay hot beyond five minutes too." She glanced at the vent in the ceiling.

"Oooohho, dahling." Madam fixed the dupatta pleats on Di's shoulder. "This is India. Here you enjoy how Indians do. Your America, what do they know about hospitality?" She jerked open her palm. "Can't even offer a free meal on flights."

"True, true," Amrikan Sir said with his mouth full, eyes fixed on the TV.

It's not like Madam ever needed a loudspeaker. Since Josna's departure though, the thunder in her voice hit new heights, her anger fits got consistent. As if it was my fault that Josna left, third maid in a row to have left in the last six months. As if it was my fault that Sir stayed out at work more and more those days.

"First Muna, then Fauzia, then Josna. Never getting Nepali girls again," she told me earlier that morning, repeating the story of their elopement. I'd come to work for Madam after Muna and Fauzia had left. "With the watchmen and drivers standing below, gupsh-upping, it takes two grocery trips for the girls to start a lafdah. Faster than Bollywood romance!" She eyed me as if warning me that she knew about Yadav. I didn't correct her; Fauzia was Bangladeshi.

I finished cooking, washing clothes, drying them out, ironing older ones, sweeping and wiping the kitchen floor for the second time, and finally the dishes, dishes that wouldn't stop piling high in the kitchen sink, a Qutub Minar of my own.

Di's wedding was four days away, and Madam was hosting another party for their families that evening. I was getting double the payment but putting up with the heat, the work, and being locked in this flat; to say it was tough would be a fucking understatement. Since Josna's departure, Madam had stopped paying for my cellphone service. She said I could use the landline but it had Caller ID that she'd monitor to make sure I wouldn't run away like her other maids. With my salary and Papa's surgery, I couldn't assure her enough I that wouldn't run away, even if I constantly thought about it, about Yadav.

My temptation to escape hit its peak on the evening before they left for Ambani Island. Josna finally called on my phone, after three weeks of not showing. I'd a few minutes left so we kept it short. She had started working for a young call-center employee and was happy in her home close to Voizone, that fancy commercial complex with huge, foreign-owned buildings, air-conditioned malls, and multiplex cinemas. Josna and I had once visited Inorbit Mall in Voizone where Madam took us to buy Diwali gifts for her family.

"Chaya Ma'am is out mostly, works some hundred hours a week so no hag watching my ass twenty-four-seven," Josna said. "Less money than Madam, but the peace! So worth it, yaar." I was happy to hear Josna's voice, knowing she was safe, imagining her jolt her head sideways as she often did when convinced about something. I was also mad with jealousy.

They left, finally. Sweetie Di's main wedding functions on Ambani Island were to last three days. Madam had taken the flat keys with her so I could let people in—the milkman, the postman, the grocery delivery guy—but I wasn't allowed to go out. I was looking forward to someone not nagging me for three days though. I was looking forward to the nights too. I collected the laundry to be done, Madam's party sarees and Sir's designer clothes strewn on their bedroom floor. I gathered the towels, the napkins, the pillow covers, the runners, the table mats. She told me she wanted all her clothes, linen and curtains to be washed while she was away. As I piled the laundry and recreated a multicolored Qutub Minar, I set aside an orange saree, Madam's favorite. She told me three times to handwash it, raising her index finger to my chin. I draped the orange chiffon with silver sparkles around me, making sure my sweat blended into the saree's floral perfume. I shut the bathroom door where the laundry pile reached for the ceiling. I still had the bed sheets and curtains from Madam's bedroom to add to the pile.

Standing in front of her dressing table, I dabbed her lipstick on my lips, making sure my saliva dried on it before I sealed it. In the mirror, I saw raw silk blackout curtains cover the huge windows, blocking light from their city on steroids, a city ever awake, a city growing wider and taller by the day, and reminding me of the jail I was condemned to. Sweetie Di would return to Mumbai to stay with Madam after six months of her wedding because her best friend from Amrika wanted to have a destination wedding in India as well, with three times the guests. I rearranged the pillows on Madam's bed. I'd collected three thousand rupees from Di's wedding alone. If I stuck around, I would easily make three times more from this other wedding. I'd heard that Amrikan desis like to have *all* wedding functions in India—so much cheaper for them. Papa needed two more months of physical therapy, his doctor had told him over his last visit. I tightened the silk bedsheet and tucked it under the mattress as I counted the tips in my head—from the mehendi, the sangeet, the cocktail party, the boat party, the bachelor party, the hen party.

My cell phone beeped. I read the text message, hearing my heart hammer my ribcage. I switched on the tiny ceiling lights like those in Voizone malls and cranked up the air conditioner in Madam's bedroom. I mean, if Shalu was condemned to life imprisonment, the least she could do was choose the cell with a view.

The bell rang. I wanted to run but I sauntered. I inhaled the crisp floral perfume of Madam's saree. I readjusted my hair bun, pulled a few strands to frame my face, and lowered my lehenga to expose my belly button. As I opened the door, I unhooked the sparkling orange palloo from the side of my waist. I let Yadav in.

SO LONG, COUSIN

WHEN DIA GOT THE invitation in the mail, she was delighted, of course, to hear that Rani's older sister, Kaajal, was pregnant with her first child and that Rani was hosting a baby shower for her. But didn't she deserve a phone call, at least for this occasion? If not from Kaajal, or other cousins in India who had not called her once since her move to the U.S., then at least from Rani, cousin closest to her age, cousin she hung out with the most in her Mumbai years? After all, they were both thirty-one, both Aries, both would pick a rose-water-infused shondesh over Godiva fudge cake, both had serially dated men with salt-and-pepper hair, both had spent childhood summers in Jaipur visiting their grandma—Dia, who was an only child to her parents, and Rani, who felt like an only child because Kaajal spent years in a boarding school at Shimla, the cousins finding in each other a sibling's companionship they longed for.

Seated on a chair in her apartment's balcony in San Diego, Dia flipped open the card. It was Rani Mittal's creation through and through: the colors, the handmade paper in silk, the seemingly standalone motifs connected by a delicate golden vine. Bronze peacocks accentuated the lime green on one side of the card, noting the date and venue for Godh Bharayee where Kaajal would be blessed by elders in the family. Silver baby bells bordered the lavender base on the other side and announced a Sangeet show following lunch at the shower. Dance performances to Bollywood were the norm at desi weddings, and these days, at engagement parties too, but Sangeet show for a baby shower? That was her first.

An orange-and-pink sky floated above the Pacific. Surfers, joggers, sunbathers, and volleyball players on the beach. A brunette twirled with two toddlers in their one-piece swimsuits. Just like Dia and Rani would twirl in their childhood years to the Rajasthani dance, ghoomar, Grandma had taught them—a dense overlap of circles they painted with different parts of their body. *Mera assi kalee ka lehenga.* An arm raised to the heavens, another lifting the edge of their skirt to expose its flair, they would kneel on one leg with Grandma, twirl, then kneel on another, circulating their free wrist to Ila Arun's flirtatious song. *Jhoom rayee banjaran / latake khayegee rey.* While Dia was the better dancer of the two, it was Rani who led, an unstated order of things, even in their college years when they'd bunk classes and twirl at Chowpatty Beach, reciting their dreams to each other—Dia, a call-center agent for Hansa Airlines and junior choreographer at Groove dance studio who was planning her escape to the U.S., Rani who was finishing up her diploma in interior design at Nima Niketan, Mumbai's elite vocational school for women—both manipulating their skirts and make-believing, both oblivious to the power of their imagination. Ten years down the road, Dia was a senior analyst at Bell Tech in La Jolla, San Diego, and Rani, executive art director for a Bollywood production magnate.

Dia slid the RSVP card in the self-addressed stamped envelope, ran the tip of her tongue over the flap and sealed it. Maybe they would twirl to Bollywood hits at a nightclub in Archipelago soon, Dia's favorite neighborhood in Mumbai, and she would ask Rani why she hadn't called once in the last eight years.

The next day, Dia got a text from Rani through a WhatsApp group called Mittal Gang: “Ok peeps, ideas here for Kaajal’s shower. Fave Bollywood numbers, color combo tips, menu-décor ideas, aur kyaa?” Her cousins responded with a yes, or different emoticons: thumb raised, hands clapping, a woman dancing in a red dress. She clicked on the group’s profile picture where her cousin sisters posed with Kaajal at her wedding in Mumbai a few years back. Dia couldn’t attend the wedding as she was working seventy hours a week in D.C. then. The other cousin she was once close to, Joohi, was also missing in the picture as she’d migrated to Dubai soon after Dia left for the U.S. Maybe her cousins in Mumbai would change the profile pic to include Dia after Kaajal’s shower, first time in eight years when they would come together as a family, something she constantly missed in the U.S., especially on festive occasions and public holidays: Christmas, Diwali, or Thanksgiving dinners, July 4th, Memorial, or Labor Day barbecues. She texted a hello to the girls.

“Ohhohoho. Look who’s here,” Kaajal texted after an hour.

Dia congratulated her on the baby.

“Hey hey hey, Lady Di. You’re alive,” another cousin texted after a few hours of silence. Lady Di, that’s how they’d started calling Dia since her migration to the U.S.

“I prefer Duchess of Sussex,” Dia texted with the emoji of a laughing face. She continued to type Bell Tech’s monthly performance report on her laptop and wondered where Rani was. No one responded to Dia’s comment.

“Wassup, yo?” Rani texted on the group chat a few hours later.

Wassup, a word new immigrants used at Bell Tech. “Nuffin. Chillin’ like a villain,” Dia texted back. She got no response.

Over the next few days, the cousins circulated jokes on Mittal Gang with double, triple, or multiple emoticons: faces laughing, winking, clapping, or a combination. Once, a cousin posted a video of a transvestite sitting in an armchair next to a host in what looked like an Indian version of The Jay Leno Show. Everyone laughed except Dia. Once again, she’d missed the joke.

On her evening run before leaving for India, Dia noticed a tree in full bloom. The guavas on it were smaller and smoother-skinned than the guavas she'd seen while growing up in India. Grandma would feed her and Rani diced guavas with black salt and red chili powder after their ghoomar sessions. She took a picture from her iPhone and posted it on Mittal Gang. No response.

The first time Dia returned to Mumbai, four years after her migration to the U.S., Rani was travelling in Europe for work. Dia was disappointed but looked forward to connecting with the rest of her extended family. The day she booked her flight to India, she called her cousins and shared her travel dates so they could meet and catch up. They'd all agreed—*yeah yeah; oh we must; definitely ré*—but when she got home, none of her cousins called or even texted her to say hello. It was an unstated order of things. Dia was the one to leave the country; she'd be the one to initiate communication and arrange visits to their individual homes in South Mumbai. Those who lived in South Mumbai never went North, just like veteran Manhattanites who'd rather drop dead than go to Queens for dinner. When Dia waited to fully recover from jet lag—a week—before calling her cousins, she'd amassed jokes that Lady Di was *so* busy with royal business. During her stay, an older cousin's son had also returned to Mumbai after finishing sophomore year at Princeton. No one in the family expected him to call or visit anyone in the family. The young man was on vacation; he deserved to do nothing in his parents's three-storied bungalow in Malabar Hill.

A week before Kaajal's shower, on her way to LAX for her flight to Mumbai, Dia texted her cousins, asking again who was free to hang and catch up in the city. She received no response. On arrival, she moved into her mother's flat in Gorgao, a new suburb in the back lanes of Voizone commercial complex where new constructions were still affordable to the middle class. Since her dad's death, she made it a point to live with Ma each time she visited Mumbai, even if she could now afford a comfortable hotel in the city that didn't remind her of her Voizone past. Ma's flat had air conditioning and a shower with hot water but Dia always took time readapting to the thin, hard mattress in her room. Besides, with newer malls transforming their residential complex into another commercial hub on steroids, with the trucks, rickshaws, and cars honking outside constantly, her recovery from jet lag took longer. After three nights, her circadian rhythm was beginning to settle, and she sent a text to Mittal Gang: "Hello from Aamchi Mumbai." Again, no response.

Since her arrival in Mumbai, barely any messages had circulated on Mittal Gang. Dia could've called her cousins, initiated communication yet again, but she wanted evidence that they too wanted to reconnect as a family. Was she asking for too much? She pushed her phone away and switched on the TV to Star News. A spiritual guru had been arrested outside Pune for running a secret brothel and a warehouse of smuggled weapons.

"Call your cousins at least once," Ma said, returning from the kitchen to keep up with the guru's scandal.

"I texted them," Dia said, taking a sip of cardamom chai. "But no response."

"You do your part then?" Ma rotated the spatula in her hand.

"I did, Ma. But. No. Response."

Dia had often had this conversation with her mother. Widowed just before Dia's migration and without a husband or son around, her middle-class mother had grown invisible to her affluent extended family. While Dia stayed abroad, bent on creating a life outside the survival rut she grew up with, her mother had grown deferential to the Mittals: her siblings, her cousins, their spouses.

"If anything happens, it's them, not you who'll be around to take care," Ma said. "Don't feed the ego more than family relations, beta."

"Family's why I'm melting in this oven, Ma." Dia wiped the beads of sweat around her lips with her wrist. Besides, it's important to *have* an ego before giving it up. This, she did not tell her mother. Nor did she remind her of family parties in her childhood when her uncles, aunts, and cousins would talk past them because their clothes were never designer, their shoes never dust-free or their voices never loud enough, voices that emerge not from your throat but from an awareness of your bank balance. What was the point? She alone had heard the voice of money in her extended family. Her mother had never noticed it; what she saw instead was the potential of support when her daughter created a life elsewhere, especially with a man. Daughters were riches on loan, after all. Dia jerked the remote in her hand and changed the TV channel.

Her mother returned to the kitchen. "Oh this child, this child, when has she ever listened to me! She wants to go abroad? I let her. Wants to date, not get married? I let her. Returns this time after three years, I don't say a thing. Firang values, NRI daughter, too important to call and say hello to family. Thinks texting is enough!" Ma kept talking aloud to herself. An odor of burnt milk filled the living room where Dia changed the TV channel again. Ma was making ghee, and as usual, she hadn't switched on the kitchen's exhaust fan.

Two days before Kaajal's shower Dia finally got a text from Rani. "Welcome to Bom, Yo."

"Yo," Dia answered, relieved to hear from her. "Where's you?"

"Dinner and catch up?"

"Yes, pleeeease."

"Indigo on Friday at seven?" Rani texted.

Dia puffed her cheeks. Indigo was in South Mumbai, closer to Peddar Road where Rani lived, but a hike from their flat in North Mumbai, more so these days with the metro construction turning the evening traffic into an endless nightmare.

"Bandra instead?" Meeting midway in the hip neighborhood would earn her time toward answering emails for Bell Tech that had piled up in her inbox.

"Got a Yogalates class until six-thirty so Bandra's tough."

"Saturday brunch perhaps?" Dia had heard so much about Café Marais at Carter Road and their eclectic menu of sweet and savory crêpes. She knew Rani loved crêpes.

"Lemme check my calendar and get back?"

Dia got no response.

On the day of the shower, St. Regis's banquet hall felt straight out of the weeklong weddings rich desis and Bollywood specialized in. A couple of hundred guests sat around lunch tables with elaborate arrangement of orchids as centerpieces that complemented the lavender, purple and mauve flowers adorning the hall's entrance. After congratulating the parents-to-be seated on a mandap surrounded by ube-colored drapes, Dia started the customary rounds to greet different members of the Mittal family. At the table where her mother sat, the aunties in the family commented on how much weight Dia had lost, how her complexion had turned darker with the Californian sun, how eagerly they were waiting for the family's next *good news*—her marriage, naturally. By the bar, the family boys, the uncles and the cousin brothers steered the conversation toward the usual suspects: Indo-U.S. comparisons, how with increasing privatization, India was bound to be the next global power, how the American empire with its inability to manufacture anything at home was bound to fall, how clueless Americans were with math and geography and downright stupid in buying giant sodas at restaurants offering free refills. Dia smiled and played along, trying hard to not be the American loudmouth who talked back to elders and embarrassed her mother at family reunions. She resisted asking them, *So, none of you are sending your kids to the U.S. for college, yes?*, knowing how hard her cousins were pushing their children to ace the SATs.

She walked to the table where her cousin sisters sat, helping themselves to jamuntinis and kababs. Rani wasn't around. *Lady Diiiiii, how you doo-in*, a cousin squealed as Dia took a seat, another faked a cough, and the rest greeted her with versions of *You don't keep in touch*. She found the language of blame familiar and recounted the number of times she'd called or texted to receive no response. After a lingering silence, the conversation turned to the weather, to each other's clothes, and the best items on the lunch menu. Dia surveyed the room and spotted Rani talking to a server at the buffet serving Indo-Chinese food. She was wearing a silver halterneck blouse and a turquoise leheria skirt bordered with zardozi embroidery. Her smoky eyes complemented a huge nose ring that rested below her lips, something Dia had seen only on women of her grandma's generation, desert gypsies, and Bollywood actresses.

Dia excused herself, pulled her georgette Anarkali dress toward her feet to hide her overused mojaris and rushed toward Rani. After the initial small talk and compliments on each other's outfit, they got into the buffet line for lunch. Rani told Dia about her recent trip to the U.S. for a movie production, how she and her colleague had spent a long weekend in Orlando, what fun they had with Disney World rides, her afternoon ritual at Starbucks for an almond croissant and a caramel frappuccino, and oh, her latest fave with U.S. restaurants, Mod Pizza, where they could choose all their toppings, they just didn't have the same variety of toppings in India. Starbucks and Mod Pizza? Dia wondered, adding mutton manchurian to her plate. Was this the cousin who'd asked her parents for dinner at Peshawari as her twenty-first birthday gift, the upscale restaurant rumored to have Hillary Clinton raving about her visit to India?

Dia hoped Rani would ask her something personal about her life abroad; they'd seven years and oceans between them, but Rani continued with her American experiences, the huge discounts for designer brands at outlet malls, makeup products at Sephora, and wow, IKEA, where you could buy your flat's furniture in one go. She especially loved the storage cubes in different sizes, so much cheaper than getting them custom-made in India.

"You know," Dia said, picking up shondesh by the dessert buffet and placing a couple on Rani's plate, "IKEA couldn't sell half the shades of purple you've got going here." She nodded at her cousin's décor and complimented her on the effort it must have taken to put it all together. Rani swayed her palm like it was no big a deal.

As they walked toward the table seating the Mittal Gang, Dia pointed to an elevated area in the hall, a temporary stage that had fuchsia drapes with bronze and silver tassels. "Where did you find those dupattas?" she asked.

"Mangaldas Market," Rani said, biting into a chili paneer.

"Love the way they fall. They've sarees in these too?"

"To wear?"

"As curtains, yaar."

Rani jolted her head backward. "Where?"

"For Ma's place. Wanna toss the beige curtains and bring life in."

"With that furniture in sun mica?" Rani stopped walking and turned to Dia. "Could be a disaster."

Dia circled her fork into the Szechuan chop suey.

"Okay, babes." Rani raised her hand toward the server offering drinks to the guests. "I am the Art and Design chick. Mixing suburban sun mica with hipster Rajasthan takes a certain—" She narrowed her eyes and rubbed her thumb against her index finger. "Impulsiveness, an eye for eclectic stuff—" She picked up a jamuntini from the server's tray. "I mean, a knack to bring in that token piece of modern furniture to make it all work.

"Above all, it takes…a don't-give-a-fuck attitude," Rani said, stirring the straw in her drink. "You have your strengths though."

"Like?" Dia picked up a Kingfisher from the server's tray.

Rani faked a cough.

"Haha."

"Relax," Rani said. "*You* are the stock market chick, the calculative type." She readjusted her nose ring. "You know, the eternal thinker."

Pukka Marwari, this one, Dia's cousins would joke about her in her Mumbai years. Maybe Rani was right. Growing up lower middle class in her parent's dingy flat in North Mumbai before they moved to a slightly bigger one in Gorgao, Dia was the calculative type. She was the kid who'd evaluate her options painstakingly before picking one, the kid who wore used clothes of her richer cousins, making sure she washed the silk ones on occasions to make them last longer, the kid who settled for a carrot-halwa cake for Diwali so she could insist on having a chocolate one from Taj Birdy's for her birthday. She was the woman who never kept in touch with men she'd hook up with over travels for work. Without the possibility of marriage, the emotional investment wasn't worth it. Most of all, after spending years disliking the corporate world, she was the one who kept ignoring her love of the arts, including dance, and stayed with consultancy gigs because they allowed her to repay her student loans, and to support her single mother. Without a rich dad to bail her out, Dia's capacity for risk, for not giving a fuck had never blossomed the way Rani's had, Rani who was the first Mittal woman to move out of her parents's home in her college years and live in an Upper Worli studio, the one to have quit her job on an impulse and vacationed in Bali for three months when she broke up with a boyfriend for the second time, Rani who never had to take up a job she didn't enjoy or pay all her bills from her own wallet. And maybe that's why when Rani screamed suddenly at one of the servers, the calculative kind in Dia knew she was in the middle of a mediocre deal, a relationship off the same page. No matter how close they were growing up in India, what stood now between them, it occurred to her, were seven years and a few oceans. Rani chose to stay rooted in the homeland with the rest of her cousins; she'd never idealize her past or indulge in immigrant fantasies of home and belonging in ways Dia did.

"How often did I tell you to serve piping hot starters?" Rani's voice thundered across the party hall.

"It's the air conditioning, Ma'am," the server passing the appetizers said. "We got them really hot from the kitchen."

"This is the third time you're serving cold food." Rani raised a chicken lollipop to his nose. "We've been coming here for five years, you know." She raised her voice too, emphasizing the math. "Send the master chef now. Let me talk to him."

"Easy, woman," Dia said, fanning her cousin's face playfully with a paper napkin. "Did you see the poor guy's face?"

"This is not your America, Lady Di." Rani took the napkin from Dia's hand and wiped her mouth. "If you tell these guys softly, they'll never listen."

Rani stormed toward the master chef who was rushing out of the kitchen. As she raised her palm to his face, he bobbed his head to her monologue, eyeing the server, who, in return, was nodding, chin lowered, ready to retreat into the kitchen. The guests around continued to eat and chat and seemed as oblivious to the scene as Rani was to her behavior toward the hotel staff. The moment reminded Dia of her white boss at Bell Tech, the ways in which he'd speak to his new employees, immigrants mostly with a heavy accent from South and East Asia. Unlike Rani, her boss—civility incarnate—would never raise his voice or his palm to an employee's face. Instead, he played the funny dude, cracking one inappropriate joke after another, much to the amusement of his alabaster colleagues, a shared humor being their go-to strategy in maintaining the unstated order of things.

By the time Dia reached the table reserved for the Mittal Gang, her cousin sisters had finished eating and were posing for a group selfie in front of the stage, three on each side with a hand on their hips and a pout as they sandwiched Kaajal between them. A cousin called Rani to join them while another chuckled aloud: *Yo behno, new profile pic for WhatsApp!* Dia swallowed a stuffed mushroom along with the lump in her throat. She turned toward the table behind her and saw her mother eating silently, sandwiched between aunties discussing the mediocre room service at The Raj Mahal on one side and their jadau jewelry on the other. She dug her fork into the shondesh, crumbling it.

Near the stage, a DJ spoke into the mike and asked for everyone's attention. He introduced the Mittal Gang to the audience and a dance performance by the cousins took over, the lyrics of Bollywood songs altered to honor the pregnant couple and their life as new parents. Stage lights emphasized the purple drapes behind the dancers in different shades. As the bronze, silver, and lime-green motifs on the fabrics flickered in and out of her view, Dia couldn't help but admire Rani's eye for color coordination and detail. In the climactic moment of the last song, Mittal women performed circular moves with different parts of their bodies, twirled throughout and invited the audience to join them.

Dia drank the last of her Kingfisher and cheered the dancers when an aunty tapped on her shoulder, pointing a finger at Rani, almost hidden by the guests dancing around her. Rani kept gesturing toward Dia, urging her to join them. It had been so long since Dia had danced in public that she shook her head, but Rani insisted. By the time Dia gave in and reached the stage, the DJ announced the event's last song. The tune from a snake charmer's flute overtook the hall—*Mera assi kalee ka lehenga*, their childhood favorite. The cousins stepped back to enclose Dia and Rani who raised an arm to the heavens and opened the flare of their dresses, lowering their head to the floor, then raising it in a repeated circular movement. To Ila Arun's husky voice serenading her skirt of eighty pleats, the duo painted circles with different parts of their body in the sequence Grandma had taught them—head, neck, hands, shoulders, belly, hands, hips, feet and hands—a familiar order of things, an effortless synchrony. The guests across the room joined the pregnant couple and the rest of the Mittals in clapping to the beat of the remixed Marwari classic and cheered the dancing duo whose synergy was lighting up the room. As the snake charmer's flute circled his tune to a dizzying climax, Dia and Rani twirled faster and faster, raising their arms and chins to the heavens as if both were reaching out to Grandma—an ethereal family reunion where no one led the other, no one read the other.

ROUTES

ONE

THE BOARDWALK ON HUNTINGTON Beach was overcrowded with locals and tourists, some walking in their wet suits with their surfboards, others playing volleyball a tourist couple on a Segway screaming in delight, cautioning the runners ahead to move away. Little in the expanse of this Southern Californian beach felt close to Belle Mare, the beach in Mauritius where Dia had spent hours eating Creole sausage and sipping coconut punch with her Californian BFF that summer, or Juhu Beach in her hometown Mumbai whose pav bhaji she'd pick every time over those in upscale restaurants. Little in Coffee Keen's jasmine tea here felt close to the subtle notes of Chinatown tea she'd buy at the Port Louis Market or the Assam green Ma would ship her from her favorite store in Mumbai's Inorbit Mall.

She looked past the notes on her computer screen at the renovated strip mall that extended on one side of HB pier: Rubio's, Oahu Poke Bar, Inca's Grill Peruvian Kitchen, Sushi on Fire, CVS, Athena Café, Tandoor India, Thai Singha. In that multicultural spirit of coastal California, she felt closer to her hometown Mumbai, or Mauritius that had felt instantly home.

The lady with auburn hair at the table across from her checked out the tattoo on Dia's arm: a woman seated on an open lotus. Eyebrows furrowed in concentration, the woman in the tattoo bent over an electric guitar; a bandana on her head held back her cascading curls.

"Bollywood rock star?" The lady with auburn hair pointed her finger at the tattoo.

"Saraswati." Coffee Keen's ceiling lights accentuated the bluish sketch on her arm. "A role model for the arts."

"In Bollywood?"

"In the Hindu pantheon."

"Indian culture's so fascinating."

Dia nodded, her reflex response to gora lines familiar from Voizone days.

"So you go to college?"

"Back to college." Dia sipped her tea, flattered like she got carded at a nightclub. "Again," she said, a little embarrassed.

"What are you studying?"

"Art history."

The woman slapped the table. "*Good* for you."

Dia took another sip, relieved she didn't have to explain things here the way she did with her family and her family-in-law-to-be: a midcareer switch to an arts program at Irvine, leaving behind six-figure gigs in corporate consultancy; nuts. She asked the lady about Orange County; she'd moved here from San Diego four months ago. The lady had grown up in Arizona, and they exchanged their desert and coastal stories. On her way out, the lady tapped Dia's arm, covering Saraswati.

"May the Lord give you all that you want to write about. Ask Him and you'll be surprised at what you're given," she said.

"What if I ask the Lordess?" Dia caressed her cup with a thumb.

"But there is no Lordess."

"How about the Goddess?" Dia didn't tell her Saraswati belonged to the feminine Holy Trinity among Hindus.

"Ah no. There's only one." The lady raised her finger. "And he is Jesus."

Dia waved goodbye to the lady, choosing to not respond. She

would save the cycle of action and reaction for her paper on Hollywood and storytelling, in progress on her computer screen. She drank the last of her tea and stared out at the restaurants of coastal California: Rubio's, Oahu, Inca, Athena, Sushi, Tandoor India, Thai Singha.

BROTHERS AT HAPPY HOUR

HAPPY HOUR ON FRIDAY at Xavier's was their favorite time of the week, a time when the brothers could take a break from work and home. The brothers weren't actually related. Their parents had left rural India around the same time, the sixties and seventies, and arrived in Southern California in pursuit of the American dream. The parents barely spoke English to mingle with other Americans, and they barely spoke to their spouses since they had arranged marriages typical of their generation—a relationship of convenience and social validation without enough shared interests. The parents spent each weekend with the other parents at Los Angeles's Indo-American Club, which they'd co-founded, and they celebrated every festive occasion together, bringing their kids along with them. In this way, the second-generation sons grew up to see each other as brothers. They'd gone to the same elementary and middle school in Los Angeles, then to the same high school and college; there were a couple of sisters here and there, but they'd gotten married once out of college and moved to other parts of the country. The only time the brothers split as a group was when they attended grad school, but they managed to meet once a month since they'd stayed within California. They got married within a couple of years from each other's wedding date, and thereafter, continued to meet once a week in downtown L.A. After chugging their second old-fashioned and discussing the fate of the Lakers for the nth time, they returned to their Friday stories.

"I mean, I've just entered home, I'm tired, working sixty-hour weeks, and before I can sit in peace for ten minutes, she tells me to pick up my jacket and shoes and move it to the closet right away," TJ said, the oldest in their group of five. He had not had a girlfriend since he broke up with his first at eighteen, so when he got married at thirty-four to a distant cousin after a month of rumored dating, everyone in his family was surprised yet relieved he wasn't gay.

"Geez," Robi said, taking a large sip of his old-fashioned. "How do you get this woman to chill?" He knew all about TJ's marriage to his super Type-A wife, the way she bossed his buddy around, how she couldn't stand clutter, how she expected him to pay for their travels, their dinners, and her shopping because that's what *real* men do.

"I mean, I make the bed, I make eggs for breakfast, I vacuum the floor every fucking Sunday, I clean up every evening after she's done the cooking but two minutes of downtime and she starts all over again," TJ said.

"Monika's the same way," Saral said. "Wants help in every motherfucking chore." Since TJ and Robi married within two years of finishing grad school, Saral caught up within ten months, proposing to one of the girls he knew from his parents' desi network. "And then, no matter what you do, it's always their criticism about what you don't do."

The brothers raised their glasses to touch each other's.

"Seriously dude. The pussy hat clubbers—" Vish said. He'd married Noor, his girlfriend from grad school. "It's like they want equality in everything but it never hits them that maybe they should split every bill fifty-fifty too." Vish told them about the Women's March in L.A. protesting the President that Noor chose to attend last month instead of joining him for his buddy's birthday. "What the fuck will all that pussy anger change?"

"Boys," Neel said in that cheerful tone he perpetually seemed to have these days. He discreetly checked the time on his watch. "Here's an idea to make life easier." He was the only bachelor in the group, the only one to have left California for college and grad school. Since he was living with his latest girlfriend, some FOB he met in San Diego a few years back, the brothers rarely saw him at their annual parties in greater L.A.: Diwali or Holi dinners, Super Bowl Sundays, July 4th or Labor Day barbecues. He made it to Xavier's that Friday because TJ had threatened to disown him as a buddy if he wouldn't for once quit his goddamned Bollywood life.

"How about a part-time maid?" Neel pushed up his shirt's sleeves to expose his athletic arms; he'd been working out twice a day. "Mine does bimonthly visits for cheap," he said.

"So the other day—" TJ said. "Her sister visits us from Solana Beach, brings homemade polenta and guess how much?" He raised his palm to the brothers. "Enough for one. And I'm telling myself, Jesus Fuckin' Christ, I take you ladies out, I pay for your shopping, I pay for your dinners, and you can't even get polenta for two?"

"Aww, come on, give Miss Lizzy a break," Robi said, stirring his old-fashioned. "It's haaaard, man, to fit polenta for two in a Louis Vuitton clutch."

The brothers laughed.

"Next time you share seafood curry with her, make sure you pay for the eleven mussels you eat," Saral said. "Show her she ain't the only math genius here." He thumped his empty glass on the table.

The brothers laughed.

"With all due respect," Neel said. "You were never into veggie food." He drew a circle on the table with his glass half-full. "Maybe her sister knew that."

"Yo bro." Robi hugged Neel lightly, turning his phone upside down to hide the screen. "You know you supposed to go with the flow here. Remember—" he whispered. "This is happy hour."

Neel chuckled, opened his palms and pushed back his elbows as if resigning to the rules of the game. Vish yelled as one of the Lakers missed a dunk. The brothers checked the score on the huge TV hanging on the wall across from them. Their conversation moved to plans for Christmas. Neel was going to spend it with that FOB in New York. Saral was going to spend it at his older brother's in Irvine, Robi and TJ would go to their parents' in Cerritos; their wives would join them, as always. When they looked at Vish, he said, "Noor's mad at me."

"What now?" TJ said.

"Because I made Christmas plans without asking her," Vish said. "Says I never ask her before making holiday plans."

TJ took a sip from his glass; Robi and Saral clapped, their eyes glued to the TV screen.

"I mean, she missed my parents' anniversary last month, missed my colleague's baby shower, missed my buddy's birthday, always having work deadlines or weekend plans of her own so I got fed up and made plans," Vish said. "I mean, she can join us, what's the problem, really? Not like I'm telling her not to."

The server stopped by. TJ circled his finger over their empty glasses. Neel's phone beeped.

"Sorry, man." Neel got up and raised his phone toward the brothers. The screen flashed a woman's face under moonlight, hidden by long, wavy hair. "I should get going."

"Whoa." TJ put his hand on his heart. "Our first hang in months and you're leaving us for her?"

"Not leaving you, bro. Saw you for some, wanna see my girl for some." Neel put a fifty-dollar bill on the table. He told the boys about his girlfriend's trip to Chicago; she'd just landed at LAX. The brothers nodded. They got up and extended their shoulder toward Neel, almost giving him a hug. They waved goodbye as he raced toward the exit, talking on his phone.

"They're living together for fuck's sake," Robi said as Neel bumped into a table and apologized to the family around. An old couple waddled after him, the woman holding the man's arm as his palm touched his belly in that classic pose of chivalry, too much for downtown L.A.

"Just how much time do you need alone?" TJ said.

"Lots before you get married," Vish said. "Almost none after five years of marriage." He raised his glass and gave it a deliberate shake. "Not even if she's the looowe of your life."

"Unless, bro—" Saral whistled. "She is the layyy of your life."

The brothers laughed.

"Let's check on this Bollywood romance after five years."

"Toojhay deck aah toh yeh jaan aah, sanammmm."

The brothers laughed.

"Yo, we going surfing on Sunday or what?" Robi asked, eyes on the TV screen.

Vish and TJ nodded.

"Dammit—" Saral jerked his head. "I gotta see her folks for brunch." He told the brothers how Monika wanted him to see her family once a month because she saw his every other weekend. "So fed up of her keeping score."

Right then, the Lakers scored against the Celtics. The men and women in the bar cheered aloud, empty glasses slammed table-tops, liquor and car commercials featuring well-endowed skinny women with full lips alternated on the TV screen. The brothers watched. They'd too much of a man in them to take their eyes off the cosmetically fixed women, not enough of a man within to take responsibility for issues in their marriage, the brothers unable to do with the women in their lives, the brothers unable to do without women in their lives. On the TV screen, a home insurance commercial followed where a white couple chilled on the sundeck of a large suburban house while their dog ran across a perfectly mowed lawn. When they weren't watching TV, the brothers glanced at the exit where Neel, stuck to his phone, ambled around the valet parking booth, laughing and waiting for his car while the old woman trailing after him adjusted her date's scarf in silence. It was like happy hour on steroids, the brothers surrounded by versions of happy between a man and a woman, each holding a mirror to their marriage, to their parents' marriage, each threatening to steer their Friday stories toward an unexpected twist.

"Awright, bro," Robi threw his arm over Saral's shoulder. "I got a solution for ya."

The brothers leaned in. Robi talked. Saral grinned. TJ gave Vish a high five. The server stopped by their table and put down another set of drinks. The brothers raised their glass to touch each other's and returned to their Friday stories, their plotlines resisting causality and change. The brothers sank into their seats. They melted back into their type.

NATURE, NURTURE

Dia, my daughter-in-law-to-be, don't care to work. Mostly, she paint mandalas on tiles, write all kinds of message on it, and have exhibition four times a year to sell her art to Laguna Beach goras. She then decorate the exhibition hall with fancy drapes and add a dance performance where she ask dancers from Orange County to join her: kathak, hip hop, salsa, Zumba, what not. All this is her job, she tell me often, which is okay, I don't mind her constant job speech as if none of us had to do real work to survive in California, except that we have a Diwali party at our house tonight and everyone want to taste the new daughter-in-law's cooking. She couldn't make samosas even if someone placed a gun to her head, she tell me more than once, shamelessly.

"Let's do a takeout, Mom. That ways, ladies can relax with the guests, just like the boys," she say today, surprise surprise. Then she rub my shoulder as if I'm a baby mourning a lost toy. "My treat."

I exhale loud. Why don't this woman get it? We're not living Bollywood life here. We have a real family to deal with, I want to tell her, but I stop myself. Not her fault if her father died when she young, her mother live alone in Mumbai, and then, Dia left her to live around the world alone for, you heard me, all kinds of jobs. What I mean is, not living with family, she don't have strong Indian values like we do. What she do have is a fine skinny butt!

"Rude to serve guests outside food," I say.

"If the food is good, no one's going to care." Dia fidget with a bonsai on the kitchen table. "Trust me," she say, plucking a few leaves attentively. She's like that, Dia. A little tinkering here with bonsai leaves, a little tinkering with music system and curtains in the living room, and life is good. She got no idea what the real world is like. Believe all world to be one big art show.

"It's about Indian culture and hospitality," I say, mixing chickpea flour with red chili powder, cumin seeds, and dice onions. "We're not goras here serving pizza and Coke and calling it a party."

"Then the boys should help us in the kitchen too?" Her chin point to the couch in the living room where they watching Laker game: my retired husband and my two sons, Dev and Neel.

"Dev and Neel work all week. They deserve a break."

"We work too and deserve a break, right, Bhabhi?" She look at Savitri, my older daughter-in-law, but Savi wave her hand backward, putting another tray of samosas in the oven. "I'm staying out of this, you two," she say.

"Neel operate for hours bending over a patient's body. Think about his back, that poor boy." Neel and Dia engaged for a year now, but it's like, I've to always remind her that her fiancé is a surgeon. She don't get it. "And then, you know," I say, kneading the spiced dough with my fist. "Man has the family's greater financial burden."

"But zero social burden. My family is oceans away." Snap come her response. Slow with her hands, fast with her tongue, Dia. "He doesn't have to go to any of my family socials," she say.

Everything with this woman is about dividing things fifty-fifty, as if their relationship is a mandala she can paint with perfect symmetry of color and design.

"Being a junior artist isn't easy either, Mom." Dia push the bonsai to the edge of the kitchen table and fake a cough just when Neel walk into the kitchen. He pick up cashews from the dry fruit bowl on the sideboard where I'm kneading dough for onion bhajias. He move toward Dia and put his chin on her shoulder.

"Why not some homemade food and some takeout? Everyone happy?" He turn to Savi who's pressing a knife against the samosas to test the crispness of the crust.

"Sure." Savi raise her palm as if she couldn't be bothered further.

"Case rested, ladies. I'll set up the patio." Neel go out, rearrange the patio table and chairs to make space, trash the grocery bags, the newspaper and old magazines, gather coffee cups, snack plates and bowls, and place them on the serving tray lying empty on the table. Dia follow him outside as if waiting for an excuse to leave the kitchen. She's carrying an overgrown money plant to our backyard where she will perfect its look while my boy will carry the unused utensils to the sink and do all kinds of ladies job, while Savi and I will fry onion bhajias, I know from experience.

Neel come inside, place the cups and bowls in the dishwasher, then hug me from behind, and whisper in my ear, "I'll call Tandoor India, Ma." He pick up more cashews from the dry fruit bowl.

You see, that's the problem. Dia cast a spell on Neel and when I turn around, I see his eyes fixed on her butt in those skinny jeans, and I know how. Dia humming some new Bollywood song while fixing the money plant. I mean, really. Who cares how long branches of the bonsai, money plant, rose plant, or the bougainvilleas have grown? Nature is supposed to be wild! Isn't there more to life than making things pretty? Relationships, nurturing others, *taking care* of family, there's a different kind of pleasure in that. These are the things I want to tell my younger daughter-in-law. But last time I tried, Neel leave office early, come to our place, and lecture me for two hours, teaching me fancy words like sexy-sum and gender-rolls. Young people these days. Just because they have education, they have money, they have love marriage, and big words for everything, they think they have all. Not worth telling them anything. So I close my eyes, my ears, my mouth, and go place onion rings covered in dough next to Savi who'll fry them.

Neel stroll out of kitchen, his palm stuffed with cashews.

"You want walnuts, Neelu?"

"Nah." He drop on the living-room couch, dialing numbers on his phone.

The dryer next to the washer in the pantry beep before shutting off. I remove all clothes, shove them in a huge wicker basket, and take them out in the patio. If she cannot cook, at least she can help fold clothes. But Dia pretend to not notice me. She now arranging my garden roses in a vase! I dump the clothes on the table and start folding them one by one. She continue humming the Bollywood song. Then, out of blue, she raise her chin, make quick sniffing sounds, and mutter something in Hindi slang, or maybe it's Marwari.

"Coconut!" She squeal. "What's Bhabhi making?" Coconut is her favorite fruit, and it show on her wrinkle-free face, complexion smooth like chocolate mousse, complexion of someone who had it too easy in life.

I raise a pair of pants to her nose. "Samosas, mini dosas, guacamole, tofu, chicken mix for tacos, macaroons, and chocolate coconut cake," I say. Instead of offering help, she fix the rose vase quickly and rush toward Savi as if to warn her of an earthquake.

I jerk down a cotton shirt to release wrinkles and watch my two daughters-in-law in the kitchen ahead. And Ram kasam, what a scene. Savi is holding the chocolate coconut cake over a tray in her mitten hands, and Dia is telling her something, nodding. The two laugh then Savi give Dia the cone filled with vanilla icing.

And there, while my beautiful Savi start cleaning cilantro—she make a killer green chutney—while frying onion bhajias on the side, Dia carry the tray to the kitchen table, sit down, cross her legs in yoga position, bring the table closer to her chest, and sketch invisible lines with her fingers over the cake. Her tongue jut out slightly, her huge brown eyes narrow with the concentration of a yogi. She raise the icing cone to the center of the cake and begin drawing a mandala.

That's when Neel walk into the kitchen again, peek inside the pantry, and grab a beer. When he step out, his head jolt as if he can't believe the scene either. Both my daughters-in-law hanging out in my kitchen and both helping make Diwali dinner. Neel move with slow, deliberate steps toward Dia, a finger on his mouth, signaling me to stay quiet. But I shake my head sideway, lip-syncing repeatedly, No, No. He must not change the scene.

FIRANG

We were all hanging at Fête in Beverly Hills, trying to have a cordial time. I was sitting next to my husband, Vishal, his shoulder grazing mine. Pinky and her husband, TJ, Vish's close friends since childhood, were seated across from us. They never held hands in public, and those days, neither did we.

"The Queen's a complex character but she's not relatable," Vish said, raising a finger.

"A ruthless father, an oblivious husband, and now, a bratty son? Of course she's relatable!" TJ had gotten louder after two dirty martinis. "Look at the King's Hand. Mr. Do Gooder, and all that. So boring." He sank back into his large cushioned chair.

I looked at the clouds and hoped it would rain. Once again, Los Angeles had a drought emergency. The patio where we were seated was surrounded by lilies, roses, bougainvilleas, and palm trees, arranged in ascending order of height.

"So Lala Land hasn't got our firang hooked on to American TV yet?" Pinky asked me. Firang, the foreigner: That's how Vish's circle of second-generation Indian American friends teased me, a fourth-generation Indo-African. They knew I'd spent my childhood in Mauritius before moving to India, France, and Northern California for school, then to Orange County once I married Vish.

"Lala Land keeps trying." I pointed at Vish. Like Pinky and TJ, Vish was raised in greater L.A. They were all *Game of Thrones* fans. They enjoyed chai tea latte too.

Truth was, I'd never been into television. And with pregnancy then, the baby was making it harder for me to sit for longer stretches so I moved as much as possible in my free time. When I wasn't on my computer web-designing for clients, I pruned the bonsai in our patio, took a walk in our neighborhood's park, or cooked fresh food to music. "Nothing beats a long day like lamb briani over an old Cassiya," I said, wondering if Pinky got it. "A sega band from our island…close to reggae," I explained, as usual, my culture to Americans, and caressed my swollen belly.

TJ coughed and tapped his chest.

"TJ's into hip-hop," Pinky said.

I took a sip from my virgin mojito.

A month before our double date, Vish and I had our baby shower in Long Beach. Pinky and TJ couldn't make it to the party as they were in Hawai'i celebrating his dad's seventieth birthday, so TJ insisted on making up for it by taking the two of us out upon their return. The dinner at Fête was our fifth outing with Pinky and TJ, and knowing my husband, we had to get along. Vish, TJ, and Pinky grew up together after their parents migrated from rural India to Southern California to start a small business—a 7-Eleven, an Indian grocery store, or a mom-and-pop motel. They might not share blood ties, but to Vish, they were family.

"My family means everything to me," he recycled his signature line when I chose to skip TJ's birthday in my first trimester to keep an appointment with a prenatal chiropractor. The baby was sitting on a nerve that gave me sciatic pain, and I used it as an excuse, no longer bothering to tell Vish why I didn't care to go to the party. We'd been through it a few times already. I'd confess the truth to him, and we'd enter a tired game of offense and defense, him accusing me of hypersensitivity toward his American family, me accusing him of insensitivity toward his African wife, both of us favoring one part of our hyphenated identity to prove a point. And just like that, a relationship of overall harmony—you could say we were your average couple; we loved each other, and we had our share of unresolved issues—would turn into a war featuring an us versus them.

"Define family," I said, holding his gaze and rubbing my belly.

Our server at Fête brought another round of tapas: baked brie, truffle fries, beef carpaccio. Vish, Pinky, and TJ were talking about the afterschool jobs they used to have at 7-Eleven with McDonald's dinners as "payment," their UC college days, TJ's younger sister's vacation in Spain, Pinky's workout routine, and their forty-year-old bachelor friend, Veer.

"Is he still seeing that lawyer chick?" Pinky asked the men. "Ali's ex?"

"On and off," Vish said. "She's not Punjabi. He claims she's not his type."

"His type is a very restricted type," TJ said. "We all know that."

Pinky laughed. Vish helped himself to a truffle fry. I wondered if anyone in the desi American trio, friends exclusively with other second-generation desi Americans, caught the irony in TJ's line.

"Rumor has it that bachelor boy is celebrating New Year in the motherland this year," TJ said.

"In Haripur, man!" Vish's voice had gotten louder as well. Haripur was Veer's ancestral village in rural Punjab, surrounded by wheat and mustard fields.

"Outside on the porch, jigging away to...Who's that guy, Bailey Sag-ooh?" Vish moved his shoulders up and down in a bhangra move. "They've got a generator now, so if the electricity goes off, nothing can stop the party this time."

I knew this story from our earlier dinner conversations. Veer had visited India once, on his tenth birthday. His parents had managed to find a good chocolate cake about fifty miles outside of Haripur, and just as Veer blew out the candles on his cake, the power went out in the entire village. Veer had thought this was how they held surprise birthday parties in India.

TJ signaled the server for another round of drinks. I stretched my neck toward Vish, wondering if the evening would drift toward another First-World rant on the Third World, but he surprised me with a twist in the plot. He told his friends how much he enjoyed the motherland on his last visit. Vish had first visited India when he was eight, for a total of ten days, all spent in their two-hundred-year-old house in a remote village in Gujarat called Deshun. The memory of mosquitos at night, power outages, giant tarantulas in the bathroom, and similar stories from his close friends had cured him of any desire to go back to India until we met at a Diwali party in Palo Alto where we went to grad school. In the shades of brown that surrounded us, we'd bonded over India, or rather, the right equation of proximity and distance to the motherland. Once we got married and paid off our student loans, we took that long-awaited trip traveling across the subcontinent together, starting with the city where my family had lived before moving to Africa, the city where I attended middle and high school—Mumbai. The new constructions and the nightlife there, the fusion-food scene in New Delhi, the Hindu-Muslim-Farsi architecture of Rajasthan, the hippie history of Goa, the Chola temples of Tamil Nadu, all had introduced Vish to a different India than the one of his childhood visit. On our last day in the motherland, before boarding our flight for California, we woke up to a stormy monsoon morning in Mumbai. We stood in silence by our room's French door, watching an Indian Ocean in fury. The gigantic waves slamming Marine Drive stirred something deep and ancestral within us, and we made love on the floor like we often did in our early months of dating. By the time we settled back into our Orange County home, I'd missed my period.

"The view of the skyline from the InterContinental's rooftop bar, man—" Vish sliced the brioche floating in melted brie. "You guys should check it out sometime. Isn't what's her name, Sweetie's bestie getting married there? Bubbly!" he said about another one of their common friends, Babita.

"Let's do it!" Pinky said. "I'm *so* hoping to go to her wedding. I could do all the shopping in India. I mean, they sell everything in Cerritos now, but the bridal boutiques in Mumbai! What I want is a badass lehenga by Sabyasachi. He designs for most Bollywood heroines these days, even Priyanka Chopra!" She pointed her martini toward TJ.

He raised his glass and said, "Cheers."

"Maybe I'll just go alone," Pinky said. "Because it's all about his family. His dad's seventieth birthday celebration in Hawai'i, his sister's baby shower in Vermont, his cousin's graduation in Chicago. My vacation ideas don't count."

I coughed into my drink; this wifely story was familiar. Vish reached for his martini and took another sip.

"They do count," TJ said. "It's just that—" He glanced at me.

"Just what?" Pinky asked.

"Come on, you know, babe. We're talking about the Third World here."

"Meaning?" I asked.

"Don't get me wrong, guys. Not that I haven't travelled to the Third World for work, but those guys—" When TJ didn't call India the Third World, he'd call Indians those guys. "The sensory overload, the population, the pollution. Mumbai is fucking crazy, man." He reached for the last slice of beef carpaccio. "And the diarrhea drama. *Every* time I eat something there." He told us the rest of the tandoori chicken story; I'd heard this one before too. The episode was at a five-star restaurant in

Mumbai. "Not like I'm not used to eating spicy food at home, still, those guys—" His eyes got wider. "They used some kind of a spice in their chicken that just killed me."

I got up, stretched my arms, and locked my hands above my head. TJ straightened his back. Our server put down the check at another table. Vish raised his hand to remind him of our drinks.

"I hear little children and women all work together there with men on construction sites," Pinky said.

"Here in America, they would never let children work like that," TJ said. "You should see the begging industry those guys have, man. Crippling little kids like that." He wiped his mouth with a paper napkin. "This one day, I'm in a rickshaw, and I see this skinny teenage kid who looks like an eight-year-old, she's nursing a baby resting on her arm, begging for money, and the mall behind her is displaying Louis Vuitton bags, and here I am, feeling so guilty about all I have." He drank the last of his martini. "And holy crap, that huge slum there. Exactly like in the movies. There's this large open ground, and that's it, that's their bathroom, and people shitting, out right in the open."

Pinky pushed her martini away. Vish squinched his eyes.

I rested my hands on my hips and bent my torso backward, my belly in TJ's face. "What did you think of all the artisanal industry in the slums?" I asked. "The leather workers, the potters, embroiderers—"

"My cab driver didn't show me that," TJ said. "Anyway, we were there at night."

The server set down three dirty martinis and another virgin mojito and asked if that would be all. Vish nodded.

"It's funny," I said. "I do exactly the same thing each time I visit my folks in Port Louis, in our *Third-World* island." I returned to my seat. "Mauritius is a part of Africa, you know," I clarified again for Americans.

TJ cocked his head.

"All I do the first three days is whine. The internet's too

slow, the traffic's too much, the heat, the air pollution, the sound pollution, poor hygiene in restaurants. And my folks, nothing pisses me off more than when they slam the door to my room after telling me, 'Let's talk once you've recovered from your firang fever, okay?' And then, three days before flying back to the U.S., I start whining about Southern California: the traffic on 405, the yoga on steroids, earthquakes, fires, fake boobs, Botox—"

Vish put his elbows on the table and leaned forward, as if eager to diffuse the tension between his friends and me. When we'd first gotten married, Vish had introduced me to TJ and his friends at one of their birthdays. The few times I hung out with them, our conversations inevitably turned to India, maybe because I was the one in the group with the longest stay in the country, maybe because it was their way to let me in through our shared connection to the motherland. Soon though, every cliché on India I'd heard from white folks in the West, my new brown family in the West was recycling—joke after joke on the motherland's lack of civilization, the poverty, the population, the heat, the dirt, the slums, especially the slums. Irritated by the end of our second dinner, I asked, "Isn't it easy to bitch about the Third World from the comforts of California's gated communities?" I chugged an oversweet rum concoction and circled my straw against the window by our table. "I mean, one more coiffed palm in this drought and I'll throw up at the Best Coast perfection."

"With due respect, sistah—" the lawyer friend working for ACLU pushed up the sleeves of his shirt and leaned forward. "Our palms ain't a lot different from those in your *Maurice*." He'd told me earlier that evening of a summer trip with his family to my island home and the blast they had at a luxury resort in Île aux Cerfs.

"My point exactly," I said, sure he was missing it.

"Oh, oh," Pinky tugged at TJ's shirt, returning to their drive in Mumbai. "Tell these guys that rat story. Please? It's my favorite."

"So I'm in the rickshaw—" TJ said. "And we see this humongous trash can where street kids are scavenging for used bottles and stuff. And there's these rats the size of a mongoose. I'm telling you, man. Everything in India feels so small and skinny, the people, the dogs, the chai glasses, but then, their rodents and insects—the biggest in the world! And we see these two rats by a huge gutter, they're dragging a dead cat."

"No fuckin' way," Vish said.

"I'm telling you, man," TJ said. "Those rodents, do not underestimate!"

I got up and rubbed my belly again. "Restroom break," I told them.

As I relieved myself in the toilet, possibilities about the rest of our evening flooded my mind. I could've declared a war against Vish—how clueless his yuppie friends were, how spineless he was in front of them. I could've preached, as I often did in a room full of Americans—couldn't they see I was the token *Third Worlder* among them? Wasn't their First-World arrogance crossing a line here? I could've listed the equations of power and privilege within the shades of brown. Hell, I could've really raised the stakes and had my husband choose once and for all, me or his friends. But we had a baby on board then, and fight or flight, that classic response in relationships, had lost its appeal. I flushed and shut the toilet door after me. The baby began kicking inside me as if prodding me to push the dinner to a higher pitch, a juicier story. I washed my hands in the sink, opened the window next to it, and sat on the bench in the ladies room. At thirty-five weeks, I was huge, and the July heat wasn't helping. With a hand on my belly, I breathed deeply as my prenatal yoga instructor had taught me to. I breathed through the discomfort and stared into the garden from the window next to me, doing my best to flow with the moment, another lesson from my yoga instructor. No epiphany appeared from the drought-struck lushness of Beverly Hills, no insight into a fresher resolution to our story, Vish and mine. I kept breathing, and when the baby calmed down, I went out for a walk in the garden.

By the time I returned to the restaurant, an hour had passed. I pretended like it was no big deal. Everyone else at our table did the same. When I sat down, Vish told me he'd ordered desserts for all of us, including mango mousse, my favorite. TJ shifted in his seat. Pinky combed her hair with her fingers.

"How's the mango mousse?" TJ broke the silence lingering over the last course of our meal.

"Fresh," I said, taking a bite. "Just sweet enough."

I tasted the dessert, trying to flow with the moment. I focused on the type of mango I was eating. It wasn't close to Maison Rouge of my Mauritian childhood nor the Alphonso of my Mumbai years, although the sweetness of the fruit felt different from the Mexican ones I ate in California.

"Sweet," TJ said. "Very nice."

"What time is it?" Vish looked at his cell phone.

Pinky leaned over the iPhone TJ was holding. "July Twenty-Fifth, already!" she said. "September Fifteenth, we're celebrating Robi's fortieth birthday at Solana Beach." Robi was another one of their common desi American friends. "You two must come, so mark your calendar."

"We'd the best Indian food there," Vish said, moving closer to me. "In a hole in the wall."

We'd gone to Solana Beach shortly after we left Northern California, got married, and moved together into our new home in Orange County. It was a honeymoon of sorts, a time when our relationship was of equals, shielded from his Southern Californian community of family and friends we'd thereafter migrate into, a larger equation of us where I'd play the eternal minority, the token immigrant. It was a time when Vish's love of me wasn't mediated by their approval of me, an approval conditional on how graciously I accepted their intolerance to difference, their self-loathing too.

"In Solana Beach, not Sunnyvale, not Cerritos," I said, mindful of my cordiality quotient.

"What was it called, something like music—" Vish said. "Sitara!" He slapped the table hard, as if relieved we're talking about other things.

"Masala crab?" TJ looked at me. "We'd been to the place while driving to my sister-in-law's last year," he said. "Seafood done in coconut milk, South Indian style, and so much lighter than the North Indian way with all that cream."

"And the sweetness of saffron rice topped with pistachio bits," I said, without looking up. "Flavor without the nasal flush of certain spices."

TJ chuckled. "Exactly."

"Noor, you've to hear about my latest culinary feat," Pinky said. "Chutney Salmon. Courtesy of desi aunty network," she whispered as if confessing a secret. "You add a ton of cumin to fresh mint chutney, spread it over a salmon fillet and seal it all in an aluminum foil." She took a last scoop of the crème brûlée. "Four hundred degrees in the oven for ten minutes, and done."

"Mmmm," Vish said, as if smelling fresh herbs in the air. He then put his arm around my waist—a rare display of spousal affection, especially in front of his people. He bent his head toward me and lowered his voice, *Eski to okay?* The only other time he'd spoken to me in Creole was on our first date. He'd walked into Palo Alto's Café Azul with an English-Kreol dictionary in hand and peppered our chat with over-rehearsed lines, cracking me up with his lack of subtlety.

"More like fifteen if you want the right texture," TJ said. "And the size of the fillet—*I'd* bake it for thirteen, actually."

Pinky exhaled for all of us to hear.

"What now?" TJ asked.

"You *had* to correct me?"

"I did not. All I said was—"

Vish rubbed my belly in a slow, attentive way, as if the two of us were alone in a room, and I closed my eyes. The baby kicked inside me again, and as I flowed into an equation of us Vish and I hadn't shared in a long time, as I heard TJ and Pinky bickering, I told myself: family.

ORDINARY LOVE

As new parents, Dia and Neel had often heard from older couples in their families that the early years of marriage are rosy rosy rosy. True colors of a couple come out once they have a child. That's when you have to adjust adjust adjust. This last line, aunties recycled more often, eyeing Dia.

Adjust, she told herself while locking the seatbelts around their one-year-old daughter, Taarini, in her child seat. Neel's dad's cousin brother was hosting the Diwali party for all of her extended families-in-law, the Samskaras, at his house in Mission Viejo. Dia and Neel hadn't recovered from their fight over their vacation plans for Hawai'i but it was their first Diwali outing with Taarini so they decided to play social that evening. While driving, Neel turned on the sports channel. He knew how much Dia disliked the male anchor's whiny voice alternating between a commentary on sports and politics with predictable quips on women celebrities. While driving in their pre-baby days, they'd mostly talk about their day at work, their latest with friends, travel destinations topping their list, post-retirement dreams, or listen to music they both enjoyed—The Beatles, Queen, U2, Bob Marley, A.R. Rahman—Neel cracking her up with his loud singing, mostly out of tune. Now, she couldn't recall the last time they'd checked in with each other, held hands while driving as they used to, or looked into each other's eyes before that habitual goodnight peck—blame it on the baby, the sleep deprivation, and the fatigue; blame it on five years of marriage and the monotony of seeing each other day after day after day, "midlife crisis" as goras would call it; blame it on the anger and frustration seething within from bumping into the same issues over and again, he accusing her of being antisocial and indifferent to his family, she accusing him of intimacy issues in marriage and an overattachment to his family.

Adjust, Dia told herself as she clasped an oxidized choker around her nape. She resisted the urge to turn down the radio volume, and the strong air conditioning in the car, another one of their frequent points of contention. Dia was always cold; Neel was always hot. Adjust. Dia wrapped a cashmere stole around her silk kurti and glared at her husband. The way he seemed focused on the road, she knew he wasn't ready to call it a truce over Hawai'i. She wouldn't either. Let him get it once and for all that his wife wasn't a pushover, the dutiful daughter-in-law, eager to oblige. She deserved downtime, and she wouldn't apologize for not wanting company during their trip, especially as a new family of three. She switched on her phone and logged into Instagram.

The party in Mission Viejo was the usual intergenerational affair, the older men discussing Trump's America or Modi's India on one side of the living room, the older women discussing the new TV production of the Mahabharata on the other side, the younger men discussing the Lakers by the bar, the younger women cooking in the kitchen, and a few others chaperoning their kids playing hide-and-seek or board games in the upper floor's living room. As Neel took Taarini out of her car seat, his family took her and started passing her around, everyone doting upon the latest family addition. Since Taarini was born, Dia had grown invisible to her family-in-law, a feeling she'd learned to welcome, especially in these large parties where she'd trouble remembering everyone's names and the ways in which they were related. She looked around for Neel's younger cousins they were both close to, Kiran, Sherry, and Dia's former roommate from her San Diego days, Maya, the one to introduce the new parents at a Halloween party in greater L.A.

After greeting different members of Neel's family, Dia sat by the base of the staircase in the living room, sipping a Kingfisher. Neel joined her with an old-fashioned, bored quite likely with the sheer number of unknown faces at the party and the absence of his younger cousins who were stuck in traffic. As they watched the Lakers game on the TV, one of Neel's older cousins sauntered toward them, a mango margarita in hand. Dia joined the small talk between the two—how California was facing yet another drought, how they never saw the new parents at Samskara parties anymore, how the turkey kababs wouldn't last, they should run for their share, how the cousin should've made more samosas, three more families decided to join them last minute.

Neel praised the crispy dough of the spinach-paneer samosas.

"The girls have been cooking for a week, you know?" the cousin said, glancing at Dia.

In the kitchen, women continued to labor over cutting boards, by the stove, the side buffet, and the sink, and in the backyard, the men hovered over a temporary bar with their drinks and appetizers in hand.

"Phew." Dia wiped the corner of her mouth with a paper napkin. "Why not have it catered next time?" she said, knowing the hosts had the ease of middle-class American families. "I know someone who does Indian food for cheap."

The cousin snickered. "In our family, we believe in helping each other." She nodded at another cousin serving chai to the guests. Dia remembered the line from the first family-in-law party she'd attended. She'd asked one of the women why Samskara ladies hung out exclusively in the kitchen at family socials while men relaxed over drinks and food, never offering help.

The woman shrugged. "It's always been this way."

Growing up in Mumbai, Dia had imagined American desis to be more liberal than those in the motherland. She was stunned to see no woman question the gendered division of labor and leisure at Samskara parties, not even those educated in America's elite schools.

"Must be nice to just sit here and enjoy yourself." The cousin eyed Dia and slurped her drink.

Dia wagged her finger between Neel and herself. "Are you telling this to us or to me?"

Neel cleared his throat. "You guys enjoyed the islands?" He asked the cousin about her family's recent trip to the Indian Ocean region.

They had to cancel two of their flights because Mauritius and Reunion were hit by a cyclone, the cousin said. So they stayed in Seychelles throughout their vacation, and boy, when has another week in paradise hurt? "Until, of course, you open your wallet," the cousin said.

Neel laughed. Dia cheered for the Lakers; they'd scored against the Clippers.

"I should see what the kids are up to," the cousin said. "Pleasure meeting you." She bowed in front of Dia. "Madam."

Dia bowed her head in return, theatrically. "Enjoy."

"Couldn't you relax?" Neel turned toward Dia, once the cousin was out of sight.

"She could've done the same."

"But it's not about her."

"When will you stop getting defensive about your people?" Dia asked. Your people, that's how she'd started calling Neel's endless extended family in Southern California, all within fifty miles of their home in Long Beach.

"I thought we were done with the Hawai'i story?" Neel said.

After three years of dating, Dia moved in with Neel in his house in Long Beach. Instead of developing her own circle of friends in the new city, almost every weekend she'd hung out with Neel at a party planned by his people: a baby shower in Newport, a birthday party in Cerritos, an anniversary party in Marina del Rey, a funeral in Irvine. There was hardly an opportunity to enjoy downtime of her own without landing into a fight with Neel who'd mansplain the importance of family roots to the uprooted immigrant in her. Three years later, Taarini was born, giving her a breather from the social responsibilities of a wife and daughter-in-law, but as soon as Dia recovered from childbirth, the cycle started all over again. Between feeding and burping the baby, changing diapers and clothes, folding laundry, washing and sanitizing bottles, and alternating night shifts with Neel, the occasional free time she had during her maternity leave was taken up by her in-laws visiting or hosting a get-together for someone or another's special occasion, Neel, desperate for fun outside the house, Dia desperate for the same by wanting to stay in and slow down, read, watch TV, or do nothing by the beach. Even when they decided to take a vacation to Hawai'i after Taarini's first birthday, a parental milestone, Neel had gone ahead and invited two cousins and their families from the Bay Area—the conversation casually came up over the phone, he told Dia afterward, who was livid about not being asked. It's not like she didn't enjoy hanging out with his people; she got along well with most. What frustrated her was Neel's need for *good times* that constantly needed Dia's presence among his people while her own family lived oceans away in India, so Neel never had to choose between his leisure and spousely duties the way she constantly had to. Worse, as a man in the role of a son or a son-in-law, he would never be judged by his family or hers in ways that a desi daughter-in-law inevitably is when she chooses to honor her needs over those of her adopted family—a gender dynamic invisible to Neel and hypervisible to Dia.

She wiped the samosa crumbs on her fingers with a napkin and pulled her hair back into a ponytail. "We *are* done," she said. "But if you can't hear sexist sarcasms from your people, don't blame me for noticing."

"Yo, babe. Can we have a drama-free evening?" Neel drank the last of his old-fashioned. "For once?"

"Cool, dude." Dia took a big sip of Kingfisher. Another one of their classic drills: If husband is upset over something, he deserves empathy. If wife does the same, ain't she a drama queen? "Me play your social Barbie," she said.

Neel stared at the Gaia Yoga commercial on TV and the ubiquitous bliss on gora faces. "I'm getting another drink." He got up and left.

"Happy hour, folks." Dia raised her beer bottle toward the elders in the living room. *Beta, try not to think so much, ekdum cool you stay,* she heard an auntie in her head.

For the rest of the evening, Neel hung out by the bar in the backyard with his cousin brothers including Kiran, who arrived without his wife, Gul, as she was travelling for work. Dia went to the backyard to say hello to Kiran. She wanted to chat longer with him but decided to stay out of Neel's sight. *Benefit of doubt, always give the other the benefit of doubt,* another auntie spoke in her head as she entered the kitchen. She placed nonalcoholic drinks on a large tray and served them to the elders in the living room: mango lassi, coconut water, watermelon and pomegranate juice. Maybe Neel's cousin sister didn't mean to be sarcastic. As she helped herself to the last coconut water resting on her tray, she spotted Maya and Sherry in the farthest corner of the living room sipping a Kingfisher. She rushed toward them and they exchanged a giddy, girlie hug.

"You surviving my cousin?" Maya asked.

"Him more than the family," Dia said. "No offense."

"Yes offense."

"Not all family, silly." Dia picked a food crumb out of Maya's hair.

"Name the victim," Sherry said.

Dia told them about their argument over Hawai'i. "Our first holiday in two fucking years! If he could have it his way, we'd have shared the honeymoon suite with his family." Dia dug a fork into the coconut meat.

"So, wait." Sherry cupped a palm under her cheek. "It's *bad* if we watch you two make a baby?"

Dia and Maya laughed.

"Welcome to the family." Maya aimed her Kingfisher toward the uncles and aunties. "It's in our blood. The Samskaras do everything in herds." She pointed to the kids running around them. "All these were likely made together too."

Dia and Sherry laughed.

"And the irony of it?" Maya took a sip of her beer. "I move to the East Coast, marry WASP men twice, but look at me now—back to my herd, sipping my Kingfisher."

"I don't mind the herd—" Dia tapped her fork against the coconut's hollow head. "As long as he remembers I've married him, not his whole family."

"*Girlfriend.* What desi chick married her husband alone?"

Dia rolled her eyes.

"Give it time. He'll eventually cut the umbilical cord," Sherry said, flashing her teeth so the women could check her smile for lipstick residue.

Dia pointed her finger toward an upper canine.

Sherry ran her tongue over it. "He's never stepped outside the herd," she said.

"Until then, deal with the roller coaster?"

"You signed up for the amusement park, babe," Sherry said. She was casually dating since she broke up with her last boyfriend three years ago.

"So buck up—" Dia scraped more of the young coconut's meat. "And suck up?" She looked at the girls.

Maya pursed her lips. Sherry dipped her samosa into mint chutney.

"I'll take the roller coaster over the low tide any day," Sherry said.

One of the family kids started screaming about being cheated. No one was allowed to hide in the laundry, didn't they already settle that?

"It's Dan." Sherry updated the two on her latest boyfriend, the one she'd been dating for four months. The two had started on a promising note but Sherry wasn't sure anymore. "It's way too smooth," she said.

"And *that's* a problem?" Dia asked. She knew how Sherry was seriously looking and ready to get married.

"Not like I dig drama," Sherry said. "But we're too similar. Hip-hop, sushi, EEtaly." She brought her fingertips to touch each other and bobbed them in front of their faces. "Even pumpkin spiced latte, we both love *without* whipped cream."

"Hm," Maya said. When it came to Sherry's love life, Maya and Dia knew she was still in love with her ex-boyfriend. The phase would pass, once she'd stop meeting the ex over Sunday brunches.

"So," Dia said, sure of what came next. "Espresso lover for you, hun?"

After catching up with Maya and Sherry, Dia returned to the kitchen to help the women who were getting ready to serve dinner to the guests. On seeing her place food items into bowls and on trays of different sizes, a cousin roasting naans over a skillet whispered into another's ear, the one dabbing ghee on the breads, "Queen Elizabeth finally enters the kitchen." The women laughed. Dia moved toward the sink and started washing the pots and pans. Through the half-open window above the sink, she could hear fragments of conversation between the men in the backyard. She spotted Neel and Kiran at a distance, their backs facing the kitchen. She shut the window partially to hide her presence, turned off the tap, and started wiping the pots dry while trying to catch the conversation between the men.

"Things getting easier?" Kiran asked Neel. He knew about the arguments between the new parents.

"Meh." Neel took a last bite of the lamb chop and rested his empty plate on the table next to them. "The bitching, the petty stuff, and shitty sleep night after night." He massaged his forehead. "Losing energy, man."

"Sleep deprivation is real. First year or so takes killer energy." Kiran also knew that Taarini, at fourteen months, was still not sleeping through the night.

Dia started rinsing the silverware. Neel told Kiran about the couple's bickering over Hawai'i. "I mean, we're living in the same house. Eat dinner together, barely go out since the baby, she's home every evening I return from work… just how much more couple's time you need?"

"Who's to measure?" Kiran told Neel about how Gul travelled to the Middle East every Christmas to see her extended family. Kiran's mother liked Gul to be in California over the holiday season as that's the only time their entire family got together. Gul worked long hours as an immigration lawyer and travelled often to the U.S.-Mexico border, especially with the separation of families these days; Christmas was the only time she could take a few days off to see her own people. "Every time, Ma and Gul—"

A cousin added cumin seeds to a pan on the stove. The seeds crackled and smoke rose. The cousin turned the vent to full speed, momentarily drowning the voices in the backyard. After adding the tempering to the dal placed in a copper kadai, the cousin switched off the vent. Dia kept rinsing glasses in the sink.

"Balancing act. Meeting midway, you know?" Dia overheard Kiran as he shook the ice cube in his drink. "We took ten years to understand boundaries, us two as a team and us with our folks, another kinda team. You'll figure your own calendar."

"How do I know we'll get there?" Neel said, pushing his linen shirt's collar toward his upper back, a familiar habit. The turquoise accentuated his salt-and-pepper hair.

"Our fights these days—" Neel exhaled.

"You won't," Kiran said. "Time alone will tell."

"Until then, keep groping in the dark?"

"Speaking of. How is the groping in the dark?"

"Rare since baby, but always good."

"Maybe a sign?"

Dia finished loading the dishwasher and switched it on. She knew well how their intimacy had changed since Taarini was born, the biggest reason fueling their fights, not the sleep deprivation, not their obliviousness toward each other's needs, not their communication down to the list of daily chores each needed the other to remember, even if it were all of it, yet above it all, their inability to truly touch each other, let the petty stuff dissolve in the play of sweat, salt, and interlocked bodies, the way it did before the baby. Dia mopped the wet floor under the sink. She took the fish tikkas a cousin had arranged on a tray to the guests in the living room. *A chair is not just a chair, it's a tree in a forest, it's a tree removed from a forest, a resting place for the tired, a challenge for the handicapped. Always, bachcha, look at a situation from multiple perspectives.*

When Dia and Neel drove home, the radio was off, Taarini was dozing, and the couple was already making small talk—something about getting out and reconnecting with the Samskaras had altered the energy between them. They talked about the kababs that stole the show, a cover band for Queen that was to play soon at Hollywood Bowl, the restaurant recommendations Neel had received for Maui. He looked at her and added, "Should we decide to go?" He told her next about the party Kiran's brother-in-law was hosting in two weeks to celebrate Gul's promotion at work. "Wanna go?" he asked.

Maya and Sherry had already told Dia about the party. Like Neel, Dia felt close to Kiran and Gul, but the girls had warned her about the older generation of Samskaras who'd be there for most, the ones allergic to younger women drinking and having fun outside the kitchen.

"I...er," she said. "Seeing a colleague for lunch, but I'll stop by later for a bit." This way, Dia could see Kiran and Gul without being stuck in the kitchen for the rest of the evening.

"Cool."

Dia was startled by Neel's neutral tone. *Family means everything to me*, how often she'd heard him lecture, each time she chose her needs over his people's. Not only had Neel spared her a full-blown spiel on relationships but offered to take Taarini with him so she could have quiet time that evening. Kiran's doing, Dia thought. Maybe she'd reschedule the lunch and show up for all of the party.

"Cool," Dia said as the CD player in the car went on. She looked past her window as Bono sang "Ordinary Love." The new parents were still not holding hands, they still had to resolve the Hawai'i issue, and if they were willing someday to risk real talk and listen, they still had to work through their issues of intimacy, boundaries, and compromise, both of them stubborn, both self-righteous and hopelessly convinced about their point of view to things. Dia lowered her car window. Outside, the evening was turning cool and fall was surrendering to winter. As they approached their driveway in Long Beach, she noticed the leaves on some trees had changed color, others had shed a few over the sidewalk. What had stayed intact through the changing season though were the rose plants in bloom, the flowers an outburst of warm colors—crimson, coral, pink and gold—their lush thorns ready to bleed you unawares.

BLUE AND BROWN

THEY DAB SUNTAN LOTION on their bodies. Lots of lotion. They dab it on their arms, legs, shoulders, backs, noses, cheeks, and other parts they want to expose to the sun. The sun, they cannot get enough of it. How they love the sun. How they fear the sun.

They read, swim or play ball, but mostly, they recline in their beach chairs or on their beach towels, sipping colorful cocktails with colorful umbrellas, staring out at the blue that sprawls before them. Sometimes, they lie on their bellies. Women unhook their bikini bras, exposing the white line dividing their freshly baked, freshly brown bodies.

Every once in a while, they rent kayaks, windsurf boards or standup paddleboards, and go deeper into the ocean. These cost way more than renting a beach chair or a beach umbrella. They don't indulge in water activities often. They are here on vacation. They want their money's worth; they are determined to do nothing. So they dab more suntan lotion on their bodies, hopeful for the right shade of brown, one that screams beach vacation once they return to the gray and the snow.

The carefully curated brown here at Kreol Sun Resort is different from the brown there, at Île Biche, an islet sold to The Raj Mahal and converted into a seven-star resort, east of

Vakvak Island. There, they rarely sunbathe, rarely read naked by the beach. There, the beach is full of water bikers, windsurfers, scuba divers, snorkelers, kayakers, parasailers, and more recently, reef walkers. There, they're on vacation too. There, they want their money's worth too. They haven't come all this way to do nothing, to lie on the beach, sunbathe, and read. They've enough sun back home. Last thing they want is to get any browner than they already are.

Sometimes, both brown parties, the natural and the artificial, hang out at Port Europa, Vakvak's capital. They've taken their resort buses to go out and experience local life. They walk around the Olympia waterfront and take photographs under the statue of Baudeloque, firang poet who made Indian Ocean islands famous across the world. They go to the market and haggle over export rejects of Ralph Lauren and Christian Dior, titillated to score a 30% discount. They stop by the food carts noted in their *Lonely Planets*, and help themselves to chicken briani, boulettes, di pain frire, gato pima, dholl puri, and sugarcane juice. They proceed to buy beach baskets, mostly imitations of cane from China, essential oils of cayenne, anise, eucalyptus, organic soaps, vanilla tea, and dark rum. Exhausted, they return to their resort buses, recline in their seats, and stare out at the Olympia waterfront where local college kids, rich ones mostly, take selfies and munch slices from the newly opened Domineau Pizza.

If they were to sit upright and look on the other side of this depot made exclusively for tourist buses, they would see beyond the commercial towers in the distance an ocean that isn't quite blue. The water here is a smoky gray from cargo ships docking from across the world, a gray that complements the soot-covered roofs and windows of dilapidated two-storied buildings nearby. I live in one of those buildings along with the janitors, cooks, laundry staff, and gardeners who work for Kreol Sun and The Raj Mahal resorts. I'm the one without a job though, the one without a government identity card. We're all brown too, but the darkest shade of brown found on this part of the world. We live in those soot-covered buildings owned by Vakvak's government who evacuated us from our islets, one sunny day. My single mother died while giving birth to me on the boat that spewed us out here.

If they continue staring northward at the gray of the ocean, they can imagine our islets on the Indian Ocean's turquoise carpet, arching in opposite directions like bindis on the forehead of a Hindu bride. Our archipelago is now closed to the world to serve as a military base. For America, England, or France—no one knows for sure, different rumors each month. Some say, our islets will be used to bomb the Middle East, others, to compete with Diego Garcia, and yet others, to lease gas and oil rights to China.

But they'll not see any of this. They're exhausted from their day's trip into local life. They recline in their bus seats, their shopping bags on their laps or under their feet, full of beach sarongs, beach baskets, essential oils, organic bath products, tea, rum.

Both buses will leave Port Europa soon. They'll exit the city square, the market, and the financial district, and enter the well-maintained country roads that will morph into the other side of the island's coast, home to tourist resorts and the ferry station to Île Biche. En route, the buses will slither through sugarcane fields. The sun will set outside; its rays will hallow the sugarcane pods with a golden aura. A double rainbow will connect purple mountains in the distance where the enslaved escaping sugar plantations made a home once; it rained earlier by the mountains today. And maybe, it's in surreal moments like these when Vakvak wears a golden, green and violet cloak sashed with double rainbows that it comes close to resembling what Baudeloque called the island once—a tropical paradise. It's in moments like these that Vakvak becomes my home too.

But they'll miss this version of paradise, reclined in their bus seats. Another paradise awaits them on their return to the resort, an all-you-can-eat buffet that will include grilled shrimp, crabs, lobsters, coconut, and lychee punch, served against the backdrop of a live sega performance. Many will return home tomorrow to the snow, to the heat, to the pollution: Australia, Sweden, France, Italy, USA, Dubai, Bahrain, India. So they nap, they snore, they reenergize themselves for a last taste of paradise, happy with their sneak peek into local life. They nap, so tired, so happy.

SHAKTI AT BRUNCH

THE SISTERS HAD MET at a party hosted in greater L.A. by one of their husbands. The sisters weren't related; they'd felt an easy connection in their first meeting which, over the years, had developed into a sisterhood stronger than the brotherhood their husbands shared. Unlike their husbands who were raised in greater L.A. and buddies since childhood, the sisters were immigrants of Asian descent who'd lived in different parts of the world before becoming American in their Californian home. Dia was originally from India, Noor from Mauritius, Malaika from South Africa, and Gul from Iran. Unlike their parents-in-law who'd migrated from rural India to the U.S. in the sixties or seventies with minimal access to English, the sisters were urban immigrants who left their motherlands decades later with fluency in more than one language, but this did not prevent their husbands at parties from joking about their parents and the sisters through the same, exaggerated Apu accent they reserved for all first-generation immigrants. The sisters joked back that their coconut husbands might protest in "Immigrants Make America Great" rallies across the country but they would never be best buds with a true FOB from the Third World, unless it involved them sharing a bed.

Besides a shared sense of humor, it was a shared culture shock of marrying into a desi American community that had connected the sisters in their early years of marriage, a second-generation's white-washed vision of the motherland—the cows, the monkeys, the population, the pollution, the slums; the disconnect their husbands faced with their parents, the former aggressively American, the latter aggressively Indian; the parental pressure ABCDs often faced toward choosing a lucrative career, and so forth. The passage of years had eased this culture shock; it had nuanced their understanding of diasporic differences. When the sisters became mothers, their adopted Californian family had become the support system that their own families couldn't offer from abroad—the former took turns to babysit and arrange playdates with community kids, a huge blessing. When it came to emotional intimacy though, the sisters had remained each other's closest confidante. And now, since their children were beyond diapers, they'd started seeing each other every Saturday, their time away from work, from domestic and social duties expected of a wife, a mother, a daughter-in-law, a sister-in-law. After sweating it out at Shakti Yoga, the token studio they knew in Orange County to have Asian instructors, they got together for brunch at the café next door, Earthen, known for its organic ingredients and a variety of bottomless mimosas.

"Perfect balance of the sacred and the profane," Dia joked as she ordered another round of mimosas for the sisters, Dia who was known in the group for her addiction to cannabis cocktails once upon a time. It was Halloween weekend so she removed different kinds of mustaches from her purse and set them on their table for each to choose. By the time they'd worked through half of their meal, their conversation had moved beyond their yoga session, the L.A. fires, U.S. congresswomen, to a vent on marriage and men, a chat they could indulge in only with each other.

"He litters the whole place, and when I ask him to pick up his clothes tossed on the floor, his classic drill—" Dia continued, pressing a dandy's mustache against her upper lip. "I tell you nothing when you leave the spices on the kitchen counter. Do you see me whine about it?" she said in a deliberately bass voice, running her fingers through the slender mustache sliding beyond her cheeks into an upward curve. "Ain't quite the same thing, bro—" She returned to her own voice. "A: The spices are on the counter while I'm cooking, not after I'm done. And B: Do mind the pig's sty. Just when you do, have the balls to say what bothers you. Don't wait for an argument five years down the road to bring up the garam masala."

The sisters laughed.

"Men," Gul said, stroking her goatee. "Got the lamest sense of analogy." She squeezed her nose and lips, making sure the mustache and the little beard didn't fall off her face. "It's like them saying: stop whining about your third-degree vaginal tear in labor. 'I bruised myself the first time I shaved too. Do I ever whine about it?'"

The sisters laughed.

"Ladies," Noor said, checking out her face with a short mustache à la Hitler in her iPhone's camera. "If you think his littering is annoying, wait till you've to live with your parents-in-law."

Malaika shuddered; Dia, a steady exhale.

"No, seriously," Noor said. "The moment he hits home and sees Mommy, Baby Boy regresses into a three-year-old." She tied her hair with a scrunchie from her wrist. "He plops into that couch facing the TV, waits to be fed, burped, changed, and cleaned by Mommy before falling asleep until you jolt him awake cuz it's time for all to hit the sack."

"As the saying goes," Dia said. "Brown boys will be brown boys."

The sisters patted their mustaches. They raised their glasses to touch each other's.

"When it's not getting coddled by Mama, it's going blind in front of the fridge or the closet, yelling he can't find the eggs or the socks," Malaika said, stroking her mustache, three times as big as Hitler's and almost covering her mouth. "But mind you, those eyes work fine while checking out the football score on TV or the neighbor's Botoxed ass," she said.

"In Baby Boy's defense—" Dia said, dabbing almond butter on her pancake. "The neighbor needs the validation of his fine eyes just as much, now that she's had her nails and hair done for the nth time *and* caught up with the Kardashians."

The sisters knew about the flirting between Malaika's husband, Veer, and their neighbor, a stay-at-home mom of three who married a banker and spent hours each week in beauty salons, her carefully groomed appearance her token source of personal power, one they'd seen her wield around men.

"Frankly, let Baby Boy flirt and feed his ego—" Dia said as she removed the rosemary twig from her grapefruit mimosa. "As long as you get to flirt with that hottie coworker of yours." She took a sip of her drink. "Win-win for all."

At dinner dates after their marriage, Dia had started noticing how often her husband Neel's eyes wandered toward pretty women in the restaurant, how he took an unusual amount of time working out and getting ready for work on some days, while he couldn't bother to shower or use a deo on others, the number of gifts he received from his female patients, never receiving any from his male ones. While this had her jealous in their early years of marriage, these days, she found herself blessing any woman who'd sign up for the long haul with him; she knew how clueless he was to feminine psychology, once the honeymoon phase was over.

"Sure, fair play, you right, you right—" Malaika reached for her gluten-free scone. "Although which working mother of toddlers has time to chase dick *or* the priority to figure if she got game?"

"True that," Noor said, finishing her seafood crêpe.

"I mean, do you know how many fuckin' hours I spend each week on laundry alone?" She flicked the thyme off her pear mimosa. "Folding toddler clothes and linen, sorting them according to gender, sending the outgrown ones to Goodwill, saving better ones for their baby cousins." She took a large sip. "Add to it the dropping and picking up of kids from day care, getting groceries, cooking, cleaning the kitchen, bathing and changing the kids, reading and singing to them, potty training, taking them to the park, the aquarium, the zoo, the museums, to playdates, and putting them to sleep after a nine-to-four job, four times a week. And the worst part—" Another big sip.

The sisters nodded, the mustaches resting on their upper lip. In the group, Malaika was the one with the youngest marriage, with the youngest children too, a toddler boy and a girl, twins with a history of colic who'd just begun sleeping through the night.

"Since he makes three times as much and pays for day care—" Malaika continued. "He gets to puff his chest out and announce to the world he's supporting me, letting me work part-time when *I'm* the one supporting him with a free nanny before and after day care, free cook, free maid-cum-tutor for his kids, *I'm* the one supporting him in keeping his routine intact, in getting paid for everything he does so he can retire early and golf through his fifties."

"A choice you made by going off the pill, love?" Dia said, relieved she'd decided against a second child even if she often thought about it.

"A choice ah sho made, sistah," Malaika said, raising her glass. "And I wouldn't complain if he'd acknowledge once that I'm not working part-time thanks to him, but I'm now making half of what I used to while working three times as much." She drank the last of her mimosa. "Just once, I want him to acknowledge the fuckin' math, then he can chase as much Botoxed pussy as he wants."

"Damn right." Noor raised her glass to touch Malaika's. "Here's to the Holy Grail for all of us."

Malaika looked out of the window, as if drained of the energy rush yoga had given her that morning.

The sisters shot a glance at each other. They knew motherhood and marriage were pushing Malaika to the edge, and they hoped it was a phase. After all, they'd *all* been through it, the newborn to toddler years, the most difficult stage of motherhood, less for the children involved, more for the sleep deprivation, the degree of caregiving and household chores, an endless, invisible labor, the kind of pressure motherhood put on working women in the U.S. where access to domestic help was so much more expensive than in Asia and Africa, the pressure new parenting put on brown marriages of their generation too, where women were educated to seek equal division of domestic labor while men weren't taught to deliver it. What added to the experience was how few people they knew actually talked about the day-to-day reality of new motherhood. From desi aunties prodding women to have children *at the right age* to beatific covers of *Parents* magazine to mommy-baby yoga classes in OC—because, let's face it, dads deserved to pump iron alone—a mother in the stories recycled around them was an archetype of the giver with little else to elevate her life than nursing a newborn on a toilet seat while running errands at Costco or executing the perfect sun salutation with a twenty-five pounder on her back.

The server stopped by and picked up their empty plates. The café was busiest on weekends and a long line of families waited at the exit for a table. Gul gestured for the check.

"Sometimes, I think a heterosexual marriage is Mother Nature's biggest joke on womankind," Noor said, wiping her mouth with a paper napkin. She'd often envied her sister-in-law and her wife who seemed much more attuned to each other in marriage than middle-class straight couples she knew. Then again, the queer couple lived in the East Coast and visited them only for Diwali, Christmas, and Eid. How much did she know of their marital life on a day-to-day basis?

"I bet Mama Nature telling herself—" Dia said, reaching for the credit card in her purse. "Lemme put these two together, one so conditioned to take, another so conditioned to give, and have them commit to each other for life. And then, when I feel like it—" She took off her mustache and faked a guffaw. "I'll wake *her* up to the drama—" Guffaw. "While he insists on staying asleep."

"Call it the master plan of delegation," Gul said, taking off her mustache too. "I bet she going: Okay, my job with their evolution done. They so enough for each other." She ran a finger back and forth between two empty glasses. "Now, to the rest of my kids."

The sisters laughed. Malaika and Noor took off their mustaches.

"To evolution," Noor said, raising her empty glass.

"And another fucking growth experience," Malaika said.

The sisters brought their empty glasses to touch Noor's.

"To the game of her Maya," Dia said. "Narayan, Narayan," she rotated her head, imitating their yoga instructor who'd ended their class with a mini-lecture on dharma, karma, and the play of duality human beings were subject to. She didn't tell others how Narayan was her favorite shot at *zen* as a call-center agent once: The drink was made with a rum containing 87% alcohol.

"To light and dark!"

"Yin and yang!"

"Shiva and Shakti!"

"To Shakti and Shakti." Malaika said, moving away from the group's wry tone to a serious one.

"To Shakti," the sisters echoed.

Malaika held out her palms facing up, a goodbye ritual from their yoga class that the sisters performed at brunch before going home. They joined their hands in a circle, closed their eyes, inhaled and exhaled slowly, *letting go of all that didn't serve them*, their instructor's favorite line. They let go of the frustrations and the disappointments that build up in long-term relationships so geared in one party's favor, and as they released their resistance—momentarily—to a game of power, they let in the light, the good. They inhaled the validation that they weren't alone on the road, for it wasn't a rocky road that was hard to walk on, it was the feeling that one walked it alone. In, out, in, out, focus. They inhaled gratitude for companionship, the kind they received in their friendship, the kind they received in marriage too, remembering the good moments they shared with their partners, the laughter, the lovemaking, the festive occasions, a greater extended family they'd co-created, and the children in it, their highest reward. When the mind wandered, it often projected what awaited them at home: another pile of dishes to be done, another set of clothes forgotten in the dryer, another episode of extramarital flirting to be ignored, another set of in-laws visiting for dinner, another request of their favorite meal from the kids, no no, leftovers won't do, or maybe, for a change, a word of appreciation from their spouse, even a heartfelt hug. When the mind wandered, they played a detached audience to the train of thoughts; they let it pass, as their instructor had taught them to. Light, dark, light, dark, in, out, in, out. A warm current tickled their interlocked palms, a circle of energy expanded around them. The sisters inhaled an openness to the present moment, untainted by their setbacks of the past or their expectations for the future. They exhaled a game of fiction the human mind specialized in, a game of distilling the messiness of life into a story with selective details, a game of action and reaction moving toward a resolution the ego needed to feel safe. They exhaled storytelling, they inhaled life.

Dia squeezed Malaika's palm who in returned pressed Gul's who repeated the same for Noor, a signal for the ritual's closure. The sisters focused on the coil of energy warming up their spine, another kind of power, and the only one they knew to leash the mind. They unlocked their heated palms, opened their eyes, and with a collective exhale, they let go.

VICTORIOUS

WHEN I TURNED SEVENTY-FIVE a few years back, both my children moved out of Southern California—*for good*, my daughter even joked—and fearing I may not have many years ahead of me—I feel it in my body these days—I decided to write the story I've always wanted to: the story of my journey from India to America. When I took my manuscript to publishers, they said that immigrant stories aren't in fashion anymore; they wanted something original. I told them every story is an immigrant story so how to write something original? I mean, I remember how much my children cried the first few nights of their lives, adapting to our world, missing home, the sounds and smell of their mama's womb, the ability to float freely in a fluid space instead of sleeping with flat back on a crib mattress. Aren't we all born immigrants? To this, two publishers agreed, still they said, it's not what you say, but how you say it. They advised me to tell my story like a Hollywood movie, make more drama and scenes, show not tell, take lessons for good English, sin tax and what not. I told them frankly I'm not interested in competing with Hollywood or the Queen's English. I just want to share my story for the children of immigrants like me, and there are so many like me in America, a country made by immigrants. To this, they shrugged, and I decided to not bother with publishing business. Now, I tell my story whenever I can to whoever likes to listen. In the age of iPhone, iPad, and Google, most people are too busy to listen, agree, but sometimes, at the community parties my wife and I host at our house in Anaheim, our retired friends want to live their story with me, sometimes their children or their grandchildren want more details about our past. The youngest of grandchildren are my favorite audience, and when I see them seated across from my heechko, elbows on their knees, two fists holding their cheeks, urging me to start *from the beginning-beginning,* because they too want to explore new worlds, I know it's time to retell.

Like other Gujaratis in my community, I left India in 1963 with ten dollars in my pocket, a master's degree in statistics and a copy of Kabir's poems. Vishal, my one-year-old son, and Sheela, my wife, left our rented flat in Surat, Gujarat, and returned to our village Deshun, about forty miles south. When I came to America, they lived with my parents, uncles, aunts, cousins, and their children. Twenty-six members of a joint family living together under one roof—can you ever say that about gora families? Sheela helped my folks on the farm like she helped her family before marriage and my parents helped babysit in return.

Why leave home when blessed with a large close-knit family, you may be wondering. My answer—same as many of my generation. I was teaching mathematics at a college in Surat and fifteen years had passed since the British left India, but boy, they left the country in bad shape. From one of the world's richest economies in the past, the British made India one of the world's poorest countries, and this was most felt in our villages where clean water, sanitation, basic schools, and medical care was a big problem. I was lucky to have a good teaching position, still, my salary barely covered the monthly expenses for Sheela, Vish, and me in Surat—rent, utilities, and food. Besides, I didn't want to do all my life what others in my family did, live one day at a time, worrying if we would have enough food to eat at the end of each month. In Surat, I'd heard from a couple of Patel friends who returned every Christmas to Gujarat with pockets full of dollars that life is really like paradise in America—clean air, clean water, clean roads, reward for hard work, and a young President who wants more immigrants in the U.S. So I decided to give it a try too—the American dream. Of course, now with more than fifty years in this country, I know there is a thin line separating the American dream from the American nightmare; you only have to look at the current President who hates brown people and loves building walls to keep them out, but back then, I believed whatever people told me about America.

After leaving Surat, I sailed on *The Liberty* for about eight weeks with stops in African and European countries and finally reached London. There, I lived with my cousin and his wife who ran a convenience store while completing their master's. With three more roommates from Zambia, Kenya, and Uganda also working and studying there, we shared a two-bedroom flat. I helped my cousin at his store, buying and delivering provisions, playing handyman, helping enlarge the storeroom, and adding wooden cabinets. He appreciated help in physical labor as his wife was pregnant. After three months, when I was leaving for America, he gave me fifty pounds. I promised to return it to him in a year's time but he insisted I keep it. It was a big sum for both of us, and those moments never made me forget the importance of one's own community in life.

From London, I sailed for about fifteen weeks on *Dorado* and reached Washington D.C. where I stayed with another cousin and her husband, both of whom had clerical jobs at departmental stores. I borrowed from them two hundred dollars to get an education in computers—a guaranteed pathway to a good job abroad, as others had told me in India. I took lessons in BASIC at Microchip, a coaching class nearby. But computers were rare and expensive then. The coaches kept promising us they would soon have computers for a practical session. In my six-month stay, the computers never arrived and we learnt BASIC only in theory.

I needed to figure out a way to repay my loans and send money back to my family in Gujarat. Sheela wanted to buy new blankets, a sweater, and woolen socks for Vish, and a small heater for the room where she slept with him at night; he was constantly catching cold because the window didn't shut fully. My cousin brother-in-law in D.C. told me then that he had a Punjabi friend running a newspaper stand in New York City. His wife's father had died in Trinidad so they needed to return to the Caribbean for funeral and pending paperwork. He was urgently looking for a replacement, and Ram kasam, I was relieved a source of income showed up! I left for New York where I took over the friend's newspaper stand but working sixteen hours a day in January cold, ooouf. I mean, I'd purchased cheap winter clothes in London but the wind chill in Manhattan, the way it sawed my bones, that I will never forget. If Vish had trouble in Gujarat's winter, how will he ever survive in this country? I often wondered while walking in snow with three pairs of socks under my open-feet sandals, all to save ten cents daily from the bus ride. One day, I slipped on my way to the subway station. Fortunately, I kept my hands on the ground so prevented breaking a bone—leg or hip. But I fell on my face, broke my glasses, and realized that breaking a bone in America or breaking your glasses—not big difference. Just as expensive. A new pair of glasses cost me three weeks of rent. Besides, there were hardly any Indian stores around so no dal available. I was too tired to cook anyway so I started eating meat because hot dogs cost five cents, two blocks away from the newspaper stand I worked, and gave me a break from pizza, my only food option then. Later, I started putting chilies inside my hotdog and developed a taste for them but the first week I started eating meat and was limping to my newspaper stand with a good amount of savings spent on my glasses, I missed my wife like crazy, especially her curry-dal-bhaat.

When I returned to the studio in Hoboken I shared with two Pakistanis and a Sri Lankan, I slept by the kitchen area and dreamt of Sheela and our joint family hanging out in sugarcane fields that surrounded our house in Deshun. Next day, I wrote to my wife that I planned on returning to India once the Punjabi was back from Trinidad. After all, what use making a life in America? I came here to escape the survival game in India but survival is so much harder without family or community to share your heart with. I mean, yes, I was living with Asians for most time, people I knew through family or friends, but we rarely spent time together, most of us working sixteen hours a day, and once home, too tired to do anything but sleep.

Sheela wrote back and repeated, as she would often in her letters, that I'd to stick around for Vish. A cousin's son was bitten by a snake in Deshun when he was pissing out in the open. One distant relative had died in childbirth and another of pneumonia. Our villages were still without decent doctors, not like Delhi or Mumbai, and most schools continued to have students sit on the floor to study. Even if we moved back to Surat, we'd return to the same fate—high rent, no savings. *One day at a time, Jeetu*, she ended the letter each time with a different poem from Kabir. *The melody of love swells forth, and the rhythm of love's detachment beats the time*—I remember my favorite.

My wife, Sheela. I first met her at a poetry session on Kabir at Gujarat University when she was a first-year and me a third-year-degree student. It's in exchanging his poems that we shed our mutual shyness and fell in love. Were it not for her faith and iron strength in those letters—I can show you, I've preserved them all—I know I wouldn't have lasted in this country.

Back in New York where I was selling newspapers, I came across a job opening in the classified section and got a statistician's job at Rudy's departmental store. My degree in Statistics and training in BASIC came very useful here and working indoors felt like a big promotion. This job was only five days a week, so I took up another job driving a taxi on weekends from a Nigerian desi who was looking for help so he could take classes at adult school. I was desperate to experience freedom that comes without constant debt. I was still lonely and homesick but at least not freezing crazy like before.

In two years, I paid off my loans and got an offer from Los Angeles where a couple of Patel students had opened three motels. My cousin was married to one of them, and she told me that weather in Southern California was very nice—one sweater mostly enough. My cousin and her husband needed a helping hand and you know how gora labor always expensive so I said yes and moved to East L.A. where I helped manage their motel, hung out with other Patels from India and Africa, and learned more about motel business. At first, driving on huge freeways scared me but thank God I'd previous experience driving taxis in New York, unlike other desis who had to spend a lot of money taking lessons. Another year passed and I was able to borrow some money again from my Gujarati family and friends in America. I decided to start a mom-and-pop motel close to Knott's Berry Farm in Orange County and applied for Sheela's and Vish's Green Cards under family category.

This is probably the day most clear in my memory of those early years in America—the day I welcomed my wife and son at LAX airport. Sheela was wearing a rani-pink bandhani sari, neatly pleated and pinned on her shoulder, and my son was wearing a cream pajama-kurta, as if they'd both dressed for Diwali. They were also wearing open-feet sandals and I felt thankful there was no fear of them slipping on melted snow in California. When I waved at them, Sheela looked at me, her eyes steady, wide. Maybe she didn't believe what she saw either—us as family in the same room again. I rushed toward them and first thing, I bent toward my son to lift him up. I couldn't believe that at four he was almost reaching Sheela's waist. But he stepped back and hid himself behind Sheela's sari, his eyes huge like his mother's. I got up and when I stood in front of my wife, I don't know what took over me. I hugged her tight, buried my face into her shoulder, and cried for the first time since I came to America. It was also the first time we hugged in public. And we just stood there for a few minutes, quiet, not moving, trying to control our tears. Vish give me a look that seemed to be wondering who I was and whether he could trust me.

On our drive back, Sheela's and Vish's eyes seemed glued to the window as they looked at the countless cars, the freeway with five lanes on each side, the speed with which everyone was driving. And you can call me a romantic fool for this but truth is, when I smelled the jasmine perfume in my car that day, something Sheela would wear for special occasions, fragrance I'd first smelled on her at Kabir's poetry session, our first "date" at Gujarat University, then at our wedding day, at our first Diwali as a couple, and so on, something told me it was going to get easier.

And in many ways, it did get easier. Together, Sheela, Vish, and I lived at our motel and managed it, split chores for its twenty rooms—Sheela cleaning rooms, toilets, and bathrooms, making beds, changing linen, me—mowing the lawn, vacuuming, plumbing, fixing broken stuff, refilling supplies, taking phone calls, and bookkeeping, we both taking turns staying up at night to check in clients. By age eight, Vish started helping Sheela clean the rooms and make beds. When he was nine and cleaning the yard one day, he slipped and fell into the pool while I was away shopping for supplies and Sheela was checking out clients. Fortunately, our Filipino gardener heard him crying and rescued him. Vish didn't know how to swim, and since that day, he hasn't overcome his fear of the ocean, something I still feel guilty about.

Another day, a gora customer left a lit cigarette on our mattress, and after his departure, the room caught fire. Fortunately, no one was injured otherwise we would have been sued and all our savings down the drain again. It was the seventies and we'd heard of discrimination against Indians by both white motel owners and customers, especially in Southern states. One of our friends in Atlanta even woke up a morning to find his motel's entrance door covered in swastikas and the message, *go back to your home.*

In six to seven years, we were able to pay our loans off and decided to have a second child. Ellie, our Chinese neighbor, threw a baby shower for Sheela. My wife didn't know what a baby shower was but she went anyway and when Ellie's friends gave her gifts, she still tells me how she regrets not knowing to properly thank them. When our daughter was born, we named her Radhika, but with time, started calling her Ricki like her American friends.

In another five years, we sold our motel and got a bigger, fifty-room property. Ricki started helping on weekends but cleaning bathrooms disgusted her, maybe because she'd grown up in America and neither seen our Indian village nor their open-air bathrooms like Vish did, but also because she hadn't seen our life in the first motel and its mishaps. She often complained about the stains on bedsheets of blood and semen, the smell of flushed cigarettes in toilettes, marijuana in vacated rooms, and she had an allergy to dust. We raised her with same humble values and work ethic as Vish though, and she helped at the new motel anyway.

One day, when I was at the front desk updating accounts, I heard Ricki screaming upstairs. I remembered Vish's swimming-pool incident and ran to find out what happened. I saw her standing inside a room, face buried in her hands. A woman lay dead in the bathtub, covered with water and blood that dripped from her cut wrist. The bathroom floor had a bottle of pills inside a pool of blood. I called the police immediately and was held back for inquiry at the jail. It turned out the woman had already records of extended stay in different drug rehab centers of California, and I was set free after three days. But Sheela and Vish worried like crazy about me, knowing stories of bad treatment by American police toward Indians.

For days after my return home, we would hear Ricki wake up screaming at night and we had to slowly talk her back to sleep. We had no health insurance and no idea about therapy or counseling. Besides, we couldn't afford any of this anyway. But after that suicide incident, Ricki never came to motel and we never insisted. We hired a Guatemalan man for help instead, and in the next decade, we had a good staff of Latino helpers, people very similar to us—strong family values, strong work ethic.

Few years after we bought the bigger motel, Vish got into UCI for college and then went to Stanford for MBA. At Stanford, he met his wife, Noor Patel; she was of Indian origin but was born in Madagascar and raised in Mauritius. We were delighted to know that he'd fallen in love with a Gujarati girl but then he told us she was Muslim! To add to this, our friends kept warning us how Europeanized girls did not have the same values as us. Our daughter-in-law spoke French and Creole outside of English and Gujarati, since she'd spent few years studying in France before migrating to America. Sheela and I had worries about all this but over time we got to know Noor, and frankly, in the way she cared for both of us, she was closer to the daughter I imagined having than my own daughter, Ricki.

After finishing their MBA, Vish and Noor married and started living with us in Anaheim, expanding our motel business, buying and selling properties, and forcing us to retire in the next few years. Meanwhile, Ricki was finishing up college at USC, so after graduation, we wanted her to get a Masters and get married. But she insisted she wanted a break from school, went to Thailand where she taught English for three years. When she returned to California, her behavior looked quite changed. She didn't move back with us, and insisted on living on her own at Venice Beach while working at a nearby bookstore.

By then, I was the director of Indo-American Society in Orange County where I helped with fundraising for Gujarati publications, giving donations to temples, and setting up scholarships for Asian American Studies in Californian colleges and universities. I was seen as ideal man for community service, yet I worried about my own family falling apart. As Vish and Noor got busier with the motel business, they travelled often for work. Ricki, in her turn, wouldn't call home for days, refusing to meet any guys we tried to set her on dates with. Worse thing—Vish and Ricki often got into fights over her future, especially after Ricki's friend, Makeda, visited our house one day, just before Ricki moved to her own apartment in Venice Beach. Makeda was African American with short hair dyed purple, wearing a leather jacket, and came on a big bike like Harley Davidson. In our community, we'd never seen a woman ride a manly bike and Vish made some joke that upset Ricki quite a bit. At twenty-six, she finally applied to graduate schools—MBA, she told us—and we believed her until another big fight happened between her and Vish.

One evening, we were going to have a Diwali party and had invited several desi families to our house. After a long time, my whole family would be present with me—neither Noor nor Vish were travelling that season and Ricki had driven home from Venice. Sheela and Noor had been working in the kitchen all day to make traditional Gujarati food for guests: sreekhand, puri, khaman, curry-dal-bhaat. At the party, Vik was planning to introduce Ricki to one of his business partner's friends, a Gujarati physician working at Cedars-Sinai, and if they hit it off, they could take it a step further toward marriage. We'd calmly suggested this to her once while having dinner, not that we would force her anyway into marrying him. That day, early in the morning, Ricki took her laptop and left for a café nearby. She returned home hours later, her hair cut short to the point that she almost looked bald.

"Just when are you going to start behaving like a woman?" Vish was telling her when I entered the living room from the backyard. On seeing me, he nodded at Ricki's skinny upper arm with a tattoo she'd gotten made in Venice. Two feather pens crossed like the alphabet V with lines reading: *Thou shalt not die / There will be memory / left behind*. Below the V, a name in cursive writing that looked like "Sapphal"; it meant victorious like my own name, Jeetendra. Personally, I don't like tattoo on girls but this was my Ricki so I never said anything. Just to keep peace in family.

"And what *is* womanly?" Ricki said.

"You are not wearing those clothes for the party." He pointed to the sleeves rolled up on her black shirt tucked inside skinny black jeans. "And better cover that tattoo."

"You're not the boss of me." Ricki threw the mail she was carrying in one hand at him. Vish opened the envelope and read the letter.

"So that's what she's up to now," he said, passing me the letter. I read it—an acceptance letter with scholarship to NYU's Art History program. I didn't know then one could get a degree by studying historic art. And when Noor explained to us later that day—her best friend recently got a degree in art too—I still didn't fully get it. What kind of job would Ricki get with a historic art degree? And even if she got a job, what would she actually do?

Ricki and Vish continued to argue, she telling him how she didn't want to reveal her grad school plans until she got a full scholarship. If not, she would've gone to business school, worked a couple of years in finance, and tried later for art history.

Vish caught Ricki's tattooed arm and pressed it tight, telling her to dress up right for the party. "You've rejected six guys already."

"Just why are you arranging my marriage when you never bothered with one?" Ricki tried to wrestle out of his grip.

"If you were to bring a boyfriend home, we'd happily give up the manhunt for you." Vish said, and I patted my son's shoulder, telling him to stay calm. He let her go.

"I'm twenty-six for fuck's sake!"

Vish and Ricki started raising their voices louder, Sheela and Noor watching in silence from the kitchen, maybe because they knew it was best to not interrupt the siblings. Vish told Ricki how she needed to stop being the family's baby. Everyone around including me had spoilt her rotten. If only she'd grown up in a motel cleaning toilets and stained sheets. "The problem with you is you have it all. Never had to work for a thing," he said.

"Because work must mean breaking your back in a motel. Physical labor alone leads the path to Nirvana." She picked up the envelope.

They kept arguing, I telling them to stay calm, they ignoring my presence in the room. Vish was reminding her how she was gallivanting across the world after college instead of using her youth for education and securing a stable future—it's why Sheela and I'd spent years breaking our own back. Even with a scholarship, living in New York City would cost a fortune.

"And if I married your Gujju doc and pursued an MBA, Big Bro would help me out with grad school, right?"

"You'll recover that money in two years! But art *and* history, goddammit, it's like what, choosing double suicide—" Vish walked toward our bar. "But any fool can tell you this: You die only once."

"There're options with a degree in the arts." Noor stopped frying puris and stepped out of the kitchen. "We really don't have to be the cliché of doctor, lawyer, engineer, you know?"

"No, we don't." Vish poured Johnny Walker in a glass. "But I want her to take *some*thing seriously."

"See, I told you?" Ricki turned to Noor and picked her bag from the floor. "These guys will never get it." She rushed upstairs toward her room.

Vish took a sip of his whiskey. "So you knew all along?" He looked at his wife as if both disappointed and unsurprised. We all knew that if anyone in the family, it was Noor that was closest to Ricki.

"We need to talk." Noor wiped her hands on the apron. "After the party."

"I love her dammit, but that's the problem with twenty-six." Vish shook his glass. "She hangs out with artsy goras and thinks it's noble to starve." Another sip. "If she'd known real poverty—"

"There's more to it." Noor pulled her hair into a bun and held my son's gaze. "After the party." She returned to frying puris.

Vish emptied his glass and while I knew a fight could happen anytime again between my daughter and my son, it then looked like Vish and Noor would be fighting after the party as well, and there was little I could do to control the situation. My children arguing openly in front of us was becoming more than common for me and Sheela those days. I reminded Vish to stay cool for the evening but again, he accused me of overprotecting Ricki. And maybe he was right. I did protect my daughter from a rough life a lot more than I protected my son or even my daughter-in-law. What can I say, she was the youngest of us, and isn't it nice to see someone of your own have it easier?

Two hours passed and no sign of Ricki. Our first Diwali after a long time yet far from the family day I imagined having at home. So I stopped by the bookshelf in our living room and went to her room upstairs. "Ricku." I finally knocked. No answer. "Papa here alone. I stay by your door till you open, okay?" I sat on the floor, hopeful for the evening.

Ricki opened the door in sometime, then went back to typing on her computer. I stepped inside and looked at the posters on the wall I'd seen before—a couple of actresses from Hollywood most likely, and two more of Goddesses—one with Saraswati sitting on a lotus holding the Vedas and veena in her hands, another of a gori woman with knotted hair like you see in big museums; she was writing something on a scroll placed on her lap. Recently, Ricki had added a new poster on the wall—a scene from the Mahabharata where a transgender warrior is driving Arjuna's chariot on the battlefield. I recognized him instantly. I wondered where she managed to find a poster with Princess Amba reborn as Sikhandi to avenge Bhishma for abducting her in past life. Most paintings I'd seen of Mahabharata showed the divine hero Krishna riding Arjuna's chariot, never the male-female reincarnation of Amba. Then again, knowing my Ricki, she loved the unconventional.

"Why didn't you tell us before?" I asked her about the NYU program.

"Like anyone would support a career in the arts?" she said. "Since I've a scholarship now, I can manage on my own."

She had her back turned to me as she typed away and I sat on the armchair behind her, trying to bridge our worlds through words. Truth was, I continued to see in my daughter's world a world far away from mine—in the posters on her wall, in the tattoo on her arm, in the career she wanted for herself, a world where family was not an asset but a burden. And I wondered if what I'd worked all my life to preserve would fall apart one day, just like that, without any warning. Maybe it was best Ricki went away for the art program. Maybe the distance between my children would help them not take family for granted, just like living alone in those early U.S. years made me realize how there's no substitute for family.

"I got something to show you, Ricku." I passed her my book on Kabir's poetry, a collection I'd published over my time in Gujarat University, translating and interpreting his dohas, and talking about the history of Bhakti poetry. It was written in Gujarati, and I'd never shown my children as they did not read the language. Besides, with motel work for sixteen hours a day, Sheela and I rarely spent time with our children until they grew up understanding Gujarati basics but with no interest in learning the script. They proudly call English their language. When Ricki left for college, a Gujarati student in Asian American Studies at UCLA translated my collection into English.

Slowly slowly O mind, everything in own pace happens / The gardener may water with a hundred buckets, fruit arrives only in its season. Ricki read to herself, then kept turning the pages, eyebrows creased with concentration. She asked me questions on Bhakti poetry and Kabir; she'd once read his poems in translation by a gora scholar at USC. For the first time in months, my daughter and I were having a conversation that was about something more than food, daily routine, and weekly errands. Ricki sat opposite me with her cropped hair, her tattoo, and the lines on it, all reminding me of the stories our neighbors often told about her. But then, I remembered lines from the book she was holding: *Kabir, save the wealth that remains in this moment...*

Today, as I tell you this, things are good overall with my family, maybe because we don't live together under a roof anymore—we've become a bit like gora families ourselves. Vish and Noor moved to San Francisco few years back because they got a very nice business opportunity, and they loved the city since their Stanford days anyway. Ricki shares an apartment with Makeda in Hoboken, a city so different from when I first came to America, and very expensive too. The distance has managed to keep us close and we FaceTime every two weeks. My children visit us every Diwali, Christmas, and Ramzan Id, including Makeda who is now part of our family. And you won't believe this but last month, Ricki managed to convince an editor at a small press in East L.A. to publish my story. The book is coming out next year and the best part, they love immigrant stories and don't think my English is a problem!

That day before Diwali party though, I tried hard to not think about a resolution to the story of my family—would we stay together or fall apart? I tried my best to not ask: what happens next?

Ricki stretched her legs on her mattress, her head bent over the book. "But I still don't understand, Papa," she said. "What's with *you* and Kabir?"

This was the story I should've told my children when they were growing up, not waiting until I retire. But there are many things I should've done when they were growing up. I should've watched Vish while he cleaned the motel's yard so he would never fall into the pool. I should've not asked my daughter to clean motel rooms so she wouldn't have nightmares about that suicidal woman for years later on. I should've taken my wife out for dinner for our twenty-fifth anniversary, in fact, every anniversary, just so we could share an intimate moment between the two of us, instead of falling asleep on our couch watching TV when tired, or serving our Gujarati community when free. Most of all, I should've shut up my own community when they started spreading stories about my daughter, about her love of women and a lesbian poetess tattooed on her arm because whatever her name—Sapphal, Sappha, Sappho—or whoever my daughter loved, it was none of their damn business.

As I walked toward Ricki's bed that evening, I tried to locate in my memories, the point of origin to this story, to Sheela and my story, to the story of our ancestors for whom Kabir was a father figure. I imagined myself lying next to my daughter when she was two as if I'd all the time and energy in the world to entertain her in the evening, to tell her stories until she fell asleep, and I imagined sharing that classic father-daughter moment you see in English movies. I sat by her side, ran my fingers through her short, short hair, and began: Once upon a time.

HOMECOMING

SHOULD SHE SELL THE Mittal haveli, centuries-old house of her forefathers in India?

"In the middle of the move. Get back to you soon." Dia types her last few words to Nadia Romano, the European muralist who has offered to buy her ancestral home in Rajasthan. She switches off the computer and returns to packing the photo albums in her current home in Temecula, wanting to consider her decision for the last time.

They are strewn across the floor in her living room—rows and columns of photo albums, Dia's life in fragments. The Mumbai years, the living-out-of-the-boxes years as a corporate consultant, the Southern Californian years with the wedding album, the honeymoon album, the pregnancy album, her daughter's childhood and teenage years, and somewhere, between them all, a Karizma album, imposing with its size and the cover photo's sharp resolution, an album she'd gotten made during her last trip to Rajasthan.

Not to worry sister, they stay same for life, the sales guy at the photo studio in Jaipur had reassured her.

With her husband Neel, Dia is now moving into a smaller house in Manhattan Beach, closer to their only child, Taarini, and her family in Hermosa Beach. After living in Temecula for over two decades, this new house in Los Angeles will be the last home she lives in, Dia has decided. At her age, she no longer has the energy to wrap up a life, again.

She picks up the Karizma album and runs her palm through the cover photo: a façade of Mittal haveli in Ramgad, key port for Silk Road merchants and among the richest towns in India once, a ghost town in the Thar Desert now. This haveli of her great-great-grandfather belonged once to Dia's oldest cousin, Joohi Mittal, who sold it to another Marwari family when she needed the money to save her husband from cancer. A few decades later, Joohi was relocating to Dubai with her children, and Dia lost both her parents. With the money Dia received from selling her parents' flat in Mumbai, home to too many memories, she decided to buy the house of her ancestors from Joohi's client. Mittal haveli was a way for her to stay connected to her roots, now that she'd lived the longer part of her life in her adopted home, Southern California. It was a way for her to preserve a legacy for Taarini too, her second- and third-generation American daughter, the most uprooted of them all.

Mittal haveli connected Dia to her vocation once; it gave her reasons to fuss over that essay on the Thar Desert and its legacy in the arts—architecture, dance, painting, textiles, storytelling—she presented at job talks across American universities. It won her the tenure track teaching gig at UC Riverside with the fresh perspective she brought to Giotto—her colleagues were convinced—as she compared the Italian master's work with the frescoes of Marwari havelis in Rajasthan. This haveli reinforced ancestral pride when her American family and friends drooled over their visit to Ramgad and the surrounding Shekhawati towns, when they cheered her serpentine moves of kalbelia at dance shows in Greater L.A., asserting their fascination for desert arts. The haveli even got her family a free upgrade to their hotel's Maharaja Suite when she first visited Ramgad with Neel and Taarini.

For this haveli, Dia had used every winter break she had from teaching at UCR, driving for hours in Rajasthan after the 24-hour-long flight to India, bringing together friends, family, colleagues, and desi activists to work on the UNESCO file, drafting a plea to declare Ramgad a World Heritage Site for the number of Marwari merchant homes in one town and their centuries-old frescoes, intact for most. For this haveli, she put money aside consistently for its annual maintenance and the caretaker's salary. Over the years though, raising a family in Southern California got pricier, and those annual savings of ten thousand dollars she'd wire transfer to the haveli's caretaker got meager, even for a remote town in the Thar Desert.

Should she sell the haveli?

Nadia Romano, Moroccan Italian muralist and a friend of her UC colleague has offered to buy the haveli and restore it. She sees in the cracks of the aging structure and the chipping paint of the frescoes what local buyers don't. She wants to resume the paperwork for that UNESCO file. Dia had worked on the heritage proposal for five years before giving up on it. Taarini and her husband, Carlos, had just had a baby, and they needed Dia's help with childcare. At her age and with her professional network, Romano has the time and resources to start where Dia stopped.

Dia flips through the Karizma album and pauses at the first photograph: a close-up of a flour mill that stands unused for decades in a corner of the haveli's inner courtyard. She remembers.

Over the first visit to Mittal haveli with her family, she was showing Neel and a preteen Taarini the ancient flour mill in what used to be the kitchen area for her ancestors. While her second-generation husband looked around the house with a curiosity he rarely showed toward the motherland, Taarini followed them with a heavy gait, impassive. In Ramgad, she was without the endless questions she'd ask when visiting Mumbai or other big cities of the world; she refused to take videos. Dia ushered them into the outer courtyard's gaddi where her forefathers traded in spices, wool, and cotton with the passing caravans on the Silk Road. In a small room across from the gaddi's front door, from a floor mattress the haveli's caretaker would oversee the main entrance, the watchman's cabin, and anyone else who'd enter the house. Taarini caressed the chipping paint of a wall, as if trying to tune out her mother's commentary, as if trying to tune into the stories the courtyard itself was telling her about the ancestors, Taarini who barely knew her maternal grandparents. Dia kept playing the tour guide when Taarini sauntered toward a book piled above a few in the courtyard's corner. She picked it up with the edge of her thumb and index finger, careful not to touch the dust on the cover.

Neel walked toward Taarini and bent over the book's pages full of lists, each line beginning with numbers in parentheses. "What language is this?" he asked.

The script resembled Urdu as it seemed to start from the right side of the page. Or did it? She couldn't tell. Besides English, she read and spoke fluent Hindi—the language her parents used to communicate with her like many Marwaris of their generation; she spoke a few other Indian languages in a basic way including Marathi and Gujarati, and since the move to California, an elementary Spanish.

"Marwari, no?" Taarini asked.

Dia puffed her cheeks. No clue. The script didn't resemble Hindi. Her grandma was the only one to speak to her in Marwari but she couldn't recall seeing a Marwari script, ever.

"How old is the house?" Neel asked, walking toward the marble staircase running up to the attic.

"They say two hundred and fifty years."

"They?" He turned around.

Dia shrugged. She should've had clearer answers about her origins, a word Americans often used when talking to her—strangers in public spaces with the classic *Where are you originally from?* and in subtler ways, people in university life and the book business. When it came to the details of her past, she had partial clues only. Like other Marwaris, her ancestors had moved to Indian cities more than a century back. She was born and raised in Mumbai with neighbors from all over India, each having their own language, each meeting the other in the contaminated space of Bombay Hinglish. Her father died from cancer, her mother passed away a few years back, she had no siblings, and frankly, in her life now, she was closer to her American friends than her extended family in India. Besides, what drew her to Mittal haveli wasn't the will to reconstruct an ancestral past—she preferred other kinds of fiction—but the mural art on their house, and the neighboring ones, and the stories they told.

They stepped out into Ramgad's narrow streets. Chin raised to the heavens, Dia continued to explain the mythological stories from the half-vanished paintings on one of the sidewalls of Mittal haveli. She then asked the panwallah nearby about their house's age, grateful her Marwari was functional. The guy responded to her in broken English, despite the fluent Hindi she peppered her Marwari with, despite the bandhani tunic and leather mojaris she wore that day. Must be Neel's shorts and Taarini's tank top, she thought. She told her family to stay where they were, walked a couple of blocks toward the hardware store, and talked to the local clients in Hindi. They too responded to her in English. One guy told her that Mittal haveli was a hundred and fifty years old; another, two hundred; a woman said that the Ruia family had first purchased it from Mittals about two hundred and fifty years ago then auctioned it off to the Goenkas who resold it to the Mittals and eventually to one of their American great-grandchildren.

Dia lowers the Karizma album on her lap, fighting a rush of panic. She tries not to count the years since that first visit to Rajasthan with her Californian family. She tries not to remember the times her own people had treated her like a firang—those arrivals at Mumbai Airport, her former friends from the Voizone call center, the chaat vendors at Gorgao Market, her extended family each time she visited Mumbai, including Rani, the cousin she was closest to in her childhood years.

Taarini and her American husband, Carlos, are due with their second child in two months. With their jobs and Carlos's family in New Mexico, they suggested Neel and Dia move closer to their home in the South Bay. After all, Neel had retired and Dia was getting there too.

"This one's our last," Taarini had said, running her palm across her belly when she visited Dia and Neel in Temecula, in the house she grew up in, once she found out she was pregnant again. In Taarini's indifference to Riverside County's cacti, in her preference for cool over hot colors, in her dislike of dal-churma, Dia had searched in vain for the Marwari in her. That day though, when Taarini took her mother's hand in her own and said in a soft voice, "You and Dad are not moving to a senior citizen's community. Not with us, not with your grandkids around," and when her son-in-law threw an arm up in the air as if his wife was stating the obvious, Dia smiled. Her thirty-something American children were Marwari enough, she figured.

Dia turns the page to the next photo in the Karizma album: a close-up of their haveli's window above the main entrance. It's a jharokha—an ornate wooden frame that encloses multiple frames, including the central opening, a mini-window that allows residents to look outside while maintaining their privacy. A jharokha has been the obsession of her latest shopping sprees. Their new house in Manhattan Beach has a minimalistic art deco façade with long windows, wide just enough to let light in. The patio has a Spanish fountain installed over a large mosaic of blue and yellow tiles. All she needs to make this new house her home is a jharokha window she can install as artwork on one of the walls. She'd seen a few jharokhas at the Indian arts and crafts boutique in Cerritos, and knockoffs at Pier 1 Imports and World Market. The former were too small and the wood in the latter felt hollow and cheap.

A faux window with multiple frames that she saw at the Cerritos boutique seemed to be the perfect size but it was way overpriced. All she wants is an affordable jharokha that resembles one of the windows in Shekhawati havelis. She could easily find a deal in Rajasthan, doubly intricate and for one-third the price, if only she could convince herself to take another trip.

When did it happen? When did the thought of travelling to India become exhausting? When did her body grow too firang to put up with the water and the air quality there? In her last visit to Ramgad, she couldn't stop coughing, and even after her return to California, it took her three months to recover. When did Californians stop placing her hybrid accent, calling it British, South African, Canadian, or sort-of-Indian-but-not-quite?

So is it time to sell the haveli?

The evening of their thirty-fifth wedding anniversary, a few weeks after they'd chosen their house in Manhattan Beach. After Mumbai, Temecula was the place where Dia had lived the longest. So when they closed the deal on their new home in the South Bay, she was happy, of course, to be closer to Taarini and her family, but she'd also started losing weight. Would she ever take root? She confessed to Neel over the drive to the dinner at Taarini's, exhausted from weeks of packing her life in boxes again.

Give it time, Neel had said, and after the dinner, taken her to their new house for a surprise visit. The living room's floor needed to be changed, the kitchen awaited remodeling, but their master bedroom was ready. And on one of its walls, an anniversary gift from Neel—an intricately carved jharokha whose innermost frame enclosed a miniature painting, an androgyne dancing within a circle of fire that resembled a lotus in full bloom.

Dia ran her palm through the androgyne's four hands, the curl of their fingers into various mudras, grace incarnate. Awestruck, she asked Neel where he managed to find this complement to her cherished art collection of a dancing Shiva or Shakti she'd amassed over her visits to Rajasthan, rare miniatures that echoed yet stood apart from each other.

Neel took out a card from his wallet and extended it to her. "A pass, professor?" he said.

Dia read the details of the Indian American artist from San Francisco, then looked at her very American partner of thirty-five years as if she saw him for the first time, this left-brained surgeon husband who'd maintained a steady distance from her professional life, playing the reserved, obliging spouse in UCR faculty parties instead of the social butterfly he was in his own circle of family and friends.

"A-plus," she said, overtaken by a feeling of rootedness. Love, she thought then. Trust, she understood later.

She turns to the last photograph in the album: a fresco painting above the door of the haveli's inner courtyard. Two chubby angel figures—naked toddlers with wings and red bindis on their forehead—hover over another divine couple dancing in the forest, Radha and Krishna. This one, an original from the handful of photos inherited from Joohi, always makes her smile.

"You're wasting your time," her college bestie had warned her as she put the haveli's photographs into her handbag. "Even Wilson Academy dudes have a tough time getting into MILA."

Dia pretended not to hear. She needed to make-believe. Master of Composite Arts or an MBA in the U.S. with her boyfriend, Aziz, the only path she knew to a life beyond Mumbai's survival rut and Voizone. MCA or MBA? Little did she know how swapping one alphabet with another would change the course of her life.

After saying goodbye to her bestie, she went to Mumbai Institute of Liberal Arts half an hour early, hiding her visit from her parents and Aziz; she'd deal with them if she were offered admission. She walked around MILA campus, rehearsing her lines while checking out the students in ethnic shirts, low-waisted jeans, embroidered flats, and thick-rimmed glasses screaming trendy over nerdy. She walked to the building housing Composite Arts and knocked at the chair's door.

"Come in," an authoritative voice said.

Two women sat behind a large wooden desk whose rotund thighs sported heads of wolves, similar to those she'd seen at Victoria Museum's section on decorative arts.

"I'm Dia," she said, straightening the silk stole around her neck.

One woman pointed to the chairs in front of the desk. She was wearing a blockprinted saree, a part of it thrown haphazardly across the shoulder. Seeing the huge red bindi on her forehead, Dia figured she was the chair, Dr. Gangulee—*prima donna of the artsy-fartsy types*, her bestie had filled her in. Gangulee pointed to the other woman wearing a sleeveless churidaar. "Dr. Kulkarni, vice chair."

Dia took a seat. "I'm here to learn about the entrance exam for an MCA." She reminded Gangulee about the emails she'd sent her regarding their master's program and readjusted her feet in her sandals. Around the room, huge posters covered the walls. One showed a vase with yellow lotuses; another, broken parts of a dome-like building overlapping with body parts of elephants and people, topped with a European and an Indian royal couple; yet another of underdressed women accompanying a portly woman wearing a zari-bordered nauvari with heavy jewelry.

"These." Gangulee circled her index finger toward the posters on the sidewall. "Masters of modern Indian art. Know any?" She continued to sign forms on her desk.

Dia looked at the lotuses, elephants, royalty. Fat books with big words across the cover sat on iron shelves under them: Commedia Dell'Arte, Natya Shastra, Cubism, Surrealism, Deconstruction, Postcolonialism. Her shoulders drooped. She should've taken her friend's advice.

"Remind us of your background," Gangulee said.

"I'm a Marwari," Dia said. She'd always loved creative expression: dancing, painting, storytelling. She wanted to learn more about the MCA program at MILA, the only one in the country that allowed students to mix and match art interests, how perfect for her, she was still exploring what she most loved. "Last summer, I painted walls for one of my neighbor's flats. I usually pick geometric and floral motifs from—"

"Not personal stuff." Kulkarni waved a palm while another flipped through a book. "College background."

Dia told them about her bachelor's degree in business, the easiest way for her to continue her education while working as a call-center agent. Besides, education in the arts wasn't a concept in her family; everyone went to business school to secure a living. "Marwaris are traders by history, as you must know." She cracked her knuckles. She learned of MCA as a degree only recently from Joohi.

"Baniyas, *of course*." Gangulee looked over her Gandhian glasses. "They're our cousins. What I learn from Marwaris is to be practical," she said, stressing the "w" and "r" instead of the local pronunciation, marvaadee. "Invest time and effort only in things of use."

Dia pushed a lock of hair behind her ears. "Cliché," she wanted to tell the Bengali professor with her Oxbridge drawl. "And casteist." She kept mum.

"Only fifty percent of our students pass," Kulkarni took over. "And most are from the country's best art schools, child."

Fifty percent. Dia hadn't looked up the statistics. "One chance, Ma'am. I'd like to give it a try." She ignored her quavering voice. With a degree from MILA, she could get a well-paid job in Mumbai she would actually enjoy, stay rooted, not worry about her dad's chemo bills, Joohi kept reminding her.

"Sixty hours work week for the first year, even more for transfer students from science and business," Gangulee said. "Many drop within the first month."

Dia reached for her bag. She'd come prepared for resistance. For once, she'd listened to her friend. *Easier to cross Indo-Pak border, boss.* She removed a few withered photographs that Joohi had given her.

"Our ancestral house in Ramgad, about three hours from Jaipur," she said, passing the pictures to the duo. "This one's the front courtyard." She pointed to the portraits of Indian women in different clothing styles in the nineteenth century, including one who was wearing a saree gown. The professors leaned forward. "Desert women in Indo-Western clothes," Dia said, her shoulders thrown back. She told them about the Marwari history in Thar Desert's Shekhawati region, their trade with the passing caravans of the Silk Road, how they commissioned artists to paint havelis with the latest trends in the visual arts from across the world. She showed them another photograph of a fresco painting where angels wearing bindis hovered over a dancing Radha and Krishna.

"Pretty cosmopolitan, these artists," Gangulee said, bending over the photos.

Cosmopolitan. That's a word Dia recognized from *Sex and the City*, which she loved watching on cable. "For my master's thesis, I can study haveli paintings and the stories they tell through the performing arts," she said, surprised at the confidence in her voice. "These frescoes make Shekhawati the world's biggest open-air gallery."

"But without a foundation in the *arts*, child—" Kulkarni shook her head.

Gangulee touched Kulkarni's shoulder. "Give us a few minutes," she said, eyeing Dia as if trying to decode something.

Dia put the photos back into her bag. Thanked Gangulee and Kulkarni a few times. Minutes later, when she returned to the office, she was denied admission. On the train ride to her flat in Mumbai, she hunched over her phone and texted Aziz. Yes, she was on her way to the Indo-American Student Association. It was known to help Indians get into MBA programs in the U.S., including Stern, Kellogg, and Anderson. *Array, if you get into one of those, you're set for life*, her Voizone colleagues would often tell her.

Dia closes the Karizma album and wipes the dust off the cover. The movers will be in Temecula tomorrow and they'll finish moving all the boxes and furniture to their house in Manhattan Beach. How she looks forward to playing with both her grandchildren. Go on regular hikes with her Californian besties, Gul, Malaika, and Noor, all uprooted like her, all in love with the region's landscape. Resume travels with Neel; they'll finally visit countries they've dreamt of discovering together, Egypt, South Africa, and China topping their wishlist. Her vacations in the past were always eaten up by the trips to Rajasthan, the UNESCO proposal, academic conferences, and research projects for UCR.

If any, this is the time to sell the haveli.

She'll use the money toward an early retirement from teaching. She'll try spending the rest of her life doing things she loves; she finally believes in the possibility, she's grateful for the luxury of choice. In the study area of her coastal-desert home overlooking the Pacific, she'll write the book she's dreamt of writing for years: "Silk Road and the Desert Arts." With its sale, Mittal haveli will be renamed Romano haveli, like many Marwari houses in Shekhawati that have been renamed after their new European owners. On the bright side, the haveli's artwork will be restored, and its new owner, like its preceding ones, is a brown woman with desert roots.

She seals the last box full of family albums: the family she was born into, the family she married into, the family she created with Neel, the family she chose for herself—her Californian girlfriends, her soul sisters. As she moves the last box into the garage, she leaves the Karizma album on the coffee table. She'll browse through it, one last time, over a slow cup of masala chai. She'll stroll through the labyrinths of memory, lounge in all the apartments and houses she's lived in, and consider, one last time, what it means to be home.

KUNDALINI

You like to believe you spared my life by letting me regale you over some thousand nights and one night. I won't tell them you were trying to save your royal name. You and that dimwitted bro of yours conspired and killed every woman in the city except Dunii and me. When the Marwari merchants came in with wool, cotton, and spices from the Silk Road and beyond, they wanted to meet the queen. No one spread rumors faster than merchants on the road, you knew. Dunii and I entertained you, we educated you, gave you and your bro a sense of progeny, cured you both of your homicidal instinct. You like to believe you spared us for you, your bro and your boys. I won't tell them that daughter of yours is the best read of your kids. I won't tell them about her storybook that surpasses my tales by some thousand nights and one night. I'll wait here in my Himalayan home. I hold the drum of creation in a hand, I carry Time in another. I'll wait for the daughter growing in my belly and for the time she won't be exiled by you and your boys, for the time she won't have a fatwa on her head for having revealed Dunii, our girls, and our take on you, your boys, and your Lord Almighty. Even if fatwas can be sexy these days, I'm told. They launch storytelling careers like little else.

You like to believe we don't have a control over our tongues. But it was you who went with your overrighteous bro to live in the forest for years, unquestioning, unrepentant of your dad's lack of control over his tongue. For years, I stayed at your palace, served your depressed dad and your demanding mothers while my sister Mithilaki left to serve you boys in the forest. And then, as if to add salt to the wound, your dad who was obsessed with honoring his unruly tongue kept moping about you boys. He was so full of you and your bro, he didn't mention Mithilaki's loyalty to you even once, forget acknowledging ever that you abandoned me. He kept drooling over your devotion for your bro while I managed your staff in the royal palace—cooks, maids, janitors, chauffeurs—and watched other couples spend nights together. Sure Mithilaki had it rough in the forest, but at least, she was getting laid. It's only when you returned home to live with us again that I realized how much I missed me-time, my years of deep sleep, the worlds I traveled in my dreams, the space in my king-sized bed without a patriarch snoring into my ear, without a patriarch imagining enemies who could sabotage his brotherly love again, without a patriarch chaperoning my leheria skirt for showing too much leg, and worst of all, a patriarch gaslighting me on my anger when a pregnant Mithilaki was abandoned in the forest because that bro of yours chose righteousness over humanity (surprise!), because that bro of yours…good Goddess, don't get me started on him again.

You now, another dude obsessed with righteousness. Mommy and Daddy spoilt the oldest among you rotten in the royal palace so the dying old man on the street that he noticed for the first time broke his heart to pieces. He decided to rescue *man*kind, find the path to freedom. And there, you decided to follow his footsteps—you too drowning in fraternal love. How quickly you forgot the promises you made to me, the wedding vows we took in front of our family, friends, and neighbors. You even forgot your son's whimpering—you never had eyes or ears for your daughters anyway—and there, you too left for the forest, sat still for days under a Bodhi tree, cursing me as I tried to stop you, as I tried reminding you of us and your children. You kept cursing me and my sisters for preventing you and your brothers from the divinity you finally attained, converting not just a good part of the East to your ideals but much of Hollywood today. Teach me, O Enlightened One, to not be bitter, to ignore how low the bar's set for your kind, and how rarely you're questioned for abandoning us. Us, neither your mistress nor your mother. Us, just wives.

And you, Messiah dear: the pimp of my story, the oldest heir to the white man's burden, the gatekeeper to literary *diversity*. How well you thrive in Hollywood where you rescue me from brown slum dogs and millionaires or civilize me on call-center speak via your Becky retired in The Best Exotic Rajasthani Hotel. The true liberals among you, of course, leave Lala Land for the worst coast. And there, in a literary hub standing tall on yet another stolen land, you return to your *mission civilisatrice*. When you don't forage for my story in your office's slush pile, you diversify your staff with a Black managing editor and a brown social media manager. You readjust your glasses over my manuscript. You take a sip of your chai tea latte—grande. With your alabaster team, you then discuss how to better my story, how to purge it of its fobby syntax, its fragmentation and staccato rhythm, its identity politics, its upward mobility, and Jesus H., its quiet domesticity. How solemnly you mediate my voice so my story may do more—pursue more character, more action, more conflict, more suffering, shut up more to show more—and become relatable to the hu-man-ity of all. John, Scott, Ernest, Raymond, and the Russians, anyone?

Last but not the least, love—you, the heart surgeon. Who can possibly be more important? So when you return home from work, and I, from painting in my studio all day, you're pissed if I ask you to take the trash out. The Lakers game is on. You deserve to relax; you're a heart surgeon. At Diwali parties, at Thanksgiving parties, at Holi and Christmas parties, I'm to cook, I'm to clean the kitchen, load the dishwasher, mop the floor, I'm to help your mother serve your ever-expanding fraternity of brothers, cousins, uncles, and granduncles. So if I ask you to come in the kitchen and give me a hand, chop the vegetables, devein the shrimp, grill the lamb, or set the dining table, you're tired, you say. He's tired, your mother says. He's a heart surgeon, she says; imagine the hours he's spent bending his back over a patient's body, my baby. Instead, I imagine the hours I've spent bending over that Long Beach port miniature I painted in my studio for eight hours straight. And I think of good-brown-girl ways to tell her: your baby's not a heart surgeon, Ma; your baby's someone born with a dick.

Shariaa, Luckun, Boddhisa, Nill, Bill, Danny, and Manny: you've reproduced yourself at such an incredible pace that we could use an army of Virgin mothers—wherever they are—to stop your population growth. Of course, I haven't gotten each detail of your life right. Of course, I've sullied your facts with my imagination. What can I say? I leave accuracy to you and your bros enamored with *His*tory. The list of your names is long, and the length of your lives longer for me to bother with realism and its delusions, I who own that ancient game of Form and Illusion. So I wait here in my Himalayan home—pregnant, playful, willfully amnesiac—choosing what you've labelled as the passive mode in your masculine drive to do, to make things happen. As I wait to birth another daughter into your world—my baby Tara, my sweet Tarini—I caress my swollen belly and twirl in bliss, knowing she'll return to her Himalayan home one day seeking me in the forms I manifest in her sleep. With a fist raised to the sky and clutching my damaru, I lift the edge of my hundred pleated skirt with another. I beat the drum of creation, I twirl. Chanting the mantra of all creation, UMAUMAUMAaaaa, I paint circles with different parts of my body: head, neck, hands, shoulders, belly, hands, hips, feet, and hands. I beat the drum of creation harder. I spin with the rise and ebb of my leheria skirt, I spin to the heat spreading in my belly. And as I pound my damaru to a dizzying climax, I command the coil of fire to climb up my spine and project into ether my next play with form.

Yours, in the dance of destruction and creation,

Shakti

ACKNOWLEDGEMENTS

Thanks to my family who formed a core from where I navigate life, and Art within, every day. To Ma for the rocksteady love and support, and for the foundation to my feminism even if you never claimed the f-word. To Didi for the inside jokes and laughter. To Jeeju for the easy trust. To Papa for the love of music. To Baba for the love of language. To Maiya and Dadi Ma for the irreverent humor. To the Poddars, the Sahs, and the desert ancestors for heritage.

Thanks to Leland Cheuk, my U.S. publisher and editor at 7.13 Books, for being the first one to take a chance on my manuscript, and for holding the space so my novel could stand on its own terms. Thanks to Rahul Soni, my editor at HarperCollins India, for offering *Border Less* a South Asian home, and to editor Amrita Mukerji for her thorough line edits. Thanks to Harshad Marathe for the beautiful art on the book's cover.

Thanks to all the teachers who shaped me as a writer. To Carmelita D'Souza and Gertrude D'Souza for fueling my love of language at an early age when it was unconscious. To my mentors at Bennington Writing Seminars for the essentials of craft and a deeper intimacy with language; special thanks here to Angie Cruz and Jill McCorkle for persistently believing in my voice, too. To my doctoral and postdoctoral mentors—Dr. Lydie Moudileno, Dr. Françoise Lionnet, and Dr. Shu-mei Shih—for pushing me to take reading seriously and for never lowering the bar; you offered the highest gift a writer can have.

Thanks to everyone who read and commented on the earlier versions of my novel's chapters in the writing workshops I took within and outside of institutions: your encouragement sustained me when self-doubt stifled me. Special thanks to desi sisters, Dr. Urmila Patil and Dr. Usha Rungoo, who read later parts of my book and offered insights while taking care of a newborn.

Thanks to the homes that have nurtured me and my creative aspirations deeply, even when I met them as a "tourist": Bombay, Mumbai, Calcutta, Mauritius, Rajasthan, the deserts and beaches of Southern California, especially Santa Monica and Huntington Beach.

Thanks to the artists I've never met but who are the literary parents to *Border Less*: François Rabelais, Édouard Glissant, Sandra Cisneros, Salman Rushdie, miniature painters of Rajasthan, and muralists of Marwari havelis in the Thar Desert. Thanks to the many writers whose work gifted me with a lineage when I struggled to figure how to write women with my history and ancestry in Anglophone literature; they include Aimé Césaire, Alice Walker, Bharati Mukherjee, Chitra Banerjee Divakaruni, Amitav Ghosh, Edward Said, Edwidge Danticat, Gloria Anazaldúa, Maryse Condé, Natalie Diaz, and wordsmiths of the past I cannot possibly ignore, Scheherazade and the Shaktis of Hindu mythology.

Thanks to my village of loved ones who took great care of my son at different moments of his baby- and toddlerhood so I could write when not raising a child: Amit, Ma, my parents-in-law, Jayshree Bhabhi, and our part-time nanny, America Camarena.

Thanks to Amit for picking up the tab one too many times so I could cut back on teaching, end my years-long pregnancy and birth a book, for being an excellent father to our son, and the co-traveler who met me at check-in every morning—come rain or shine—ready to take off.

Thanks to Ananya and Shome for choosing me as Masi and Mommy. I hope I can repay you and the universe somehow for this priceless gift.

ABOUT THE AUTHOR

Namrata Poddar writes fiction and nonfiction, serves as Interviews Editor for *Kweli* where she curates the series "Race, Power and Storytelling," and teaches literature and creative writing at the University of California, Los Angeles. Her work has appeared in *Poets & Writers, Literary Hub, Longreads, Electric Literature,* and elsewhere. She holds a PhD in French literature from the University of Pennsylvania, and an MFA in Fiction from Bennington College, and a Mellon Postdoctoral Fellowship in Transnational Cultures from UCLA.

Twitter: @poddar_namrata; Instagram: @writerpoddar